Dear Reader,

MY NAME IS ERIC KIRBY, and I am a survivor. I stayed alive, stranded and alone, for eight weeks in a land where dinosaurs ruled.

A lot of people have asked how a thirteen-year-old from Enid, Oklahoma, did what no one thought *could* be done. I've had my reasons for keeping quiet. The main one is I felt my mom and dad had been through enough, and the truth might be hard for them to take.

Last night, I told them everything. Every detail. I was right. It wasn't easy for them. But they told me not knowing had been a lot harder. It felt good to finally talk about what happened. So now I'm telling you.

This is my story. . . .

Don't miss the next
JURASSIC PARK™ Adventure!
PREY
by Scott Ciencin

Coming Fall 2001
ISBN: 0-375-81290-3

And check out these other
Jurassic Park titles now available:

Jurassic Park III Junior Novelization
Jurassic Park III Movie Storybook
Jurassic Park Institute Dinosaur Field Guide
Jurassic Park Institute Dinosaur Sticker Book

#1
SURVIVOR

By Scott Ciencin

AN ORIGINAL NOVEL
based on the motion picture screenplay
Jurassic Park III
written by Peter Buchman
based on the novels of Michael Crichton

RANDOM HOUSE 🏠 NEW YORK

Special thanks to Cindy Chang of Universal Studios and to
Alice Alfonsi, Jason Zamajtuk, Cathy Goldsmith, Lisa Findlay,
Mike Wortzman, Artie Bennett, Christopher Shea, Colleen
Fellingham, and Jenny Golub of Random House for their work on
this book.

Cover montage by Peter Van Ryzin
Iguanodon illustration copyright © 2001 by Robert Walters

www.randomhouse.com/kids
www.jpinstitute.com

Library of Congress Catalog Card Number: 00-111485
ISBN: 0-375-81289-X
Printed in the United States of America
June 2001   10 9 8 7 6 5 4 3 2

CHAPTER 1

"We've got a surprise for you," Ben said. He stretched out in the Jacuzzi he had installed at the stern of his yacht. My mom was beside him, sipping on some kind of tropical lemonade you could only get in Costa Rica. The yacht sliced through the perfect blue water off the coast. Ben's partner

in Dot.Com Engineering was at the wheel.

I sat on the edge of the Jacuzzi, waiting. I'm pretty sure neither of them could tell they had me worried. Things had been moving so fast lately. My mom and dad's separation, the move from Enid to San Diego, Ben and my mom . . .

I liked Ben a lot—he was my bud and he was everything my dad wasn't. Funny, smart, rich—a real risk-taker. But he wasn't my dad, and I didn't want to hear about a wedding.

"What kind of surprise?" I asked.

Ben took my mom's hand. "You want to tell him, honey?"

"Naw," she said. "It'd be better coming from you."

My shoulders tensed and I forced them to relax.

"Dinosaurs," Ben said. "I'm gonna show you Jurassic Park."

I whooped and hollered, leaping into the Jacuzzi. I hugged Ben and my mom. I was so excited I could hardly breathe.

Then it hit me.

"But what about all the restrictions?" I asked. "Isn't Isla Sorna off-limits?"

"I've got it all worked out," Ben said. "Provided you don't mind a little parasailing."

My mother smiled. I hadn't seen her smile and

laugh so much in years. "I told Ben how much you've always liked dinosaurs," she said. Then she gestured toward the mainland. "Scarlet macaws, toucans, white-faced monkeys—yeah, sure, all this exotic wildlife is beautiful, but what's one thing you *can't* just go to a zoo somewhere and see?"

"Dinosaurs," I answered. I was five when I got into dinosaurs. Seven when the news came that John Hammond's InGen corporation had employed genetic scientists to bring dinosaurs back from extinction using preserved prehistoric DNA. I must have watched the footage of that rex in San Diego a hundred times, and I told all my friends that one day I'd actually see dinosaurs for myself.

Most of them didn't like hearing that. In a town like Enid, big talk and big dreams usually meant big trouble. No one there liked change. At least, that's how it was for me.

To most of my friends, I was just a jock like them. A Waller Junior High Eagle—basketball, football, wrestling, you name it. I went to the Vance Air Force Base shows and watched the Wings of Blue parachute team descend as the fighters flew overhead. I cheered for the home of the 71st Flying Training Wing and said I'd love to be one of those guys someday. A real-life Top Gun.

I learned pretty quick to keep quiet about things like leaving Enid or seeing dinosaurs, except when I was with people I knew would understand.

I thought of one person I was sure *wouldn't* understand. Not about this.

"What about *Dad?*" I asked. My dad was Mr. Play-It-Safe. He loved Enid. Bingo night, tater tots, and *hey, let's check out them thar tractors in the mall!*

Yeah, *really* on that last part. Tractors in the mall. No lie.

Of course, my dad didn't *talk* like that. In fact, the last thing he said to me was, "I just want you to promise me that whatever you do, wherever you go, you'll be careful."

So I promised.

My mom took another sip of her lemonade. "Do you want me to call your dad? I mean, I think we both know what he'll say, but it's up to you, Eric. . . ."

Ben grinned. "Listen, there's no need to bother Eric's father. The Dino-Soar tour guy swears it's safe. He's been doing it for a while and never had anything but satisfied customers. And *I'm* going to be there."

I already knew what my dad would have said to that: *Sure, it's been safe until now—they've been darned lucky. But there's a first time for everything, and this Dino-Soar business doesn't sound safe to me.*

I thought about that promise I'd made to my father. Then I thought about the fact that if it were up to him, I'd not only still be in Enid, I'd be spending my *whole life* there!

I loved my dad, but he didn't exactly live for adventure. Not like me.

"Let's do it!" I said.

"I *will* tell your dad about your trip," my mom said. Then she grinned. "*After* you guys get back."

I looked to the bright blue water ahead. Somewhere in the distance lay InGen's prehistoric zoo—an island of real live dinosaurs.

I was going to see Jurassic Park.

I was going to live my dream!

CHAPTER 2

Dreams die. *People* die.

Deep down, you know things like that, but you don't sit around thinking about them, not unless something happens.

I was on the shore of Isla Sorna, my clothes torn, my arms and legs cut and bleeding. There was a whirlwind in my head. I knew there had been an accident.

TYRANNOSAURUS REX

One minute, Ben and I had been parasailing above the island, then something happened to the chartered boat towing us. I remembered going down into the trees. Branches ripping at us like claws. Crashing, screaming, tearing.

I remembered hanging there, Ben telling me everything was going to be all right, then looking at him and knowing that wasn't true. He'd been injured in the fall. Badly injured.

Ben said I should go to the beach. If rescuers in helicopters came, the shoreline was the first place they'd start looking.

He told me it would be all right again. He smiled. Then he got quiet. Even though his eyes didn't close, I knew he wasn't with me anymore.

I was numb as I made my way to the beach. I wasn't thinking about the dinosaurs then. I guess I wasn't really thinking at all.

Ben said he'd be there. He'd catch me if I fell. But we'd both fallen at the same time, and no one had caught us. I couldn't yet accept that Ben was gone—and I was stranded.

When I got to the shore, I stood near the tree line and looked out at the water. The early-morning fog had lifted and I saw the perfect blue of the sky. There were no clouds. All I saw was cool white sand and the waves turning lazily in the distance.

Suddenly, a breeze kicked up from the south and blew a horrible *stench* right at me.

I never smelled anything like it before. Imagine the worst case of b.o. possible, then multiply it by ten.

Some instinct told me to stay still. Then, out of the corner of my eye, I noticed a rex standing fifty yards away. It looked at least fifteen feet tall and about forty feet long.

Nothing that big was supposed to be walking around. *Nothing.* It wasn't *possible.*

But there it was.

Its hide was gray with dull red splotches. Its mouth was filled with six-inch-long serrated teeth. And its eyes were darker than any nightmare I'd ever had.

My dream had been to see real live dinosaurs. But I wasn't crazy. I'd assumed I would be *safe* when I saw them!

The rex swiveled its head in my direction. Then its enormous feet thumped slowly across the sand.

My entire body began to shake uncontrollably. Sweat dripped into my eyes, the blood drained from my face, and I could barely breathe.

A thousand chilling needles seemed to rip through me as my imagination flashed on a terrifying scene of the rex moving toward me in a blur, its open jaws blotting out the world as they closed over me. I could almost hear my screams echoing inside its maw as I stared into darkness and death!

I frantically looked beyond the dinosaur, praying that I would see rescue teams coming for me.

But there was nothing. No one.

Just me and the rex, which was blocking my

easy escape into the blue water. My only other escape now was the tree line, about ten paces behind me.

I had to make a run for cover. I knew it was my only chance!

But even though every impulse told me to run, I couldn't move. It was like there was another part of me that knew I'd never make it. Running would mean death. I *had* to stand and face this thing if I wanted to live.

And without a doubt I knew one thing—I wanted to live.

Maybe I couldn't let go of the fear, but I could force it—*will* it—into letting go of me. My body was trembling, but my mind was casting off the imagined nightmare and settling into a cool clarity. I began to focus on the very next thing I needed to do.

If I turned and ran, it'd probably get me before I could reach the tree line. And even if I did reach safety, the dinosaur might be able to knock down the trees to get at me.

Then again, if it knew I was standing here, why wasn't it running for me already?

It was still walking in my direction, but was it coming for me?

I had read in that book by Dr. Alan Grant, the famous dinosaur paleontologist, that the rex he'd encountered in Jurassic Park had tracked things by motion. T. rexes also hunted by scent. I hadn't moved in a long time, and I was downwind of the dinosaur.

Maybe it hadn't seen or smelled me yet. Maybe I still had a chance.

Cawwwrrr!

A gold-and-red Pteranodon swooped over the head of the rex, its huge wings flapping once. The rex growled and turned its head, chomping at the air where the flyer had been an instant before.

I jumped back several paces as the rex and I both watched the Pteranodon open its beak and skim over the water, just missing a fish that darted to the surface.

With a grunt, the rex swiveled its massive head back in my direction.

I froze again. Without moving my head, I looked at the tracks I had left in the sand.

This was just like a game I'd played back home when I was little.

Red light, green light, one-two-three!

I stayed still and looked at the waves.

A big one curled in the distance. I remembered Ben bragging that he was going to take on Salsa Brava, the world-famous forty-foot wave off Costa Rica, before we headed back to California.

But Ben was dead. And my dream was dead.

Cawwwrrr!

The Pteranodon came around again. It swung over the rex's head, a little lower this time. I didn't think for a second that the flyer was trying to help me out by distracting the rex. I figured if it had seen me, it would have wanted *me* for lunch instead of the fish.

The flyer angled down toward the water again. This time its beak snagged the surfacing fish.

Splissshhh!

I bounded back toward the tree line and nearly lost my balance in the sand.

Red light, green light—

My back slammed up against a tree, making me gasp. I grabbed its trunk to steady myself as the rex swiveled its head back.

The predator remained perfectly still for several seconds. Then its head started swaying from side to side.

What was it doing?

My hands tightened on the tree trunk.

It was *warm*, I realized. It was also leathery and seemed to have scales. Out of the corner of my eye I traced a huge belly and a long neck leading to the head of a sleeping sauropod.

I wasn't holding on to a tree trunk. My hands

were gripping the giant leg of another dinosaur!

I looked the other way and saw the longneck's tail swaying back and forth as it slept. It was something the rex could see.

Oh, no, I thought. *Stop, stop, stop . . .*

The tail settled, and the rex stared for what seemed like forever.

Grunting, the rex turned and walked away.

I couldn't believe it! I wanted to shout with excitement, but I kept it to myself, I held it in, I—

Pfffffu-fhhhhhhhhhhhhhrrrrrrtttt!

The sleeping longneck's body shuddered as it let loose a loud, smelly gust of gas.

I knew at once what had just happened. I'd read about how a plant-eater's stomach was like a gigantic internal combustion engine with a massive exhaust. That's how it broke down food and twigs and roots.

I wanted to run from the smell, but the rex was still walking away. So I had to hold my breath. I felt like I was going to choke.

Then a second gust of gas came, even *louder* than the first one.

PFFFF-HHHRRRRMMMMM!

The rex turned, roared, and charged. The longneck woke with a start. Its leg kicked out and I was sent flying facedown into the sand. I turned onto my back and saw the plant-eater rising, panicking.

The sauropod was the size of a small office building. It blotted out the sun!

Then its legs were coming down and I scrambled to my feet and ran, praying I wouldn't be crushed!

One foot landed close enough that I was hit by a sudden gust of wind and felt the ground shake. The rex roared again, and I saw it coming as I raced for the tree line. I targeted a pair of trees that were thick and close together. Too close for the rex to fit through.

Cahhhrrr!

Looking over my shoulder, I saw the Pteranodon swooping toward me. It looked like a small fighter plane coming in for a strafing run.

I dove between the trees, and the flyer crashed into them. Then the rex was there, grabbing the dazed flyer in its maw, chomping and slapping it back and forth like a dog with a chew toy.

The predator spit the flyer out and ran after the longneck, which was thundering down the beach.

I turned and ran, heading as deep into the jungle as I could.

I didn't look back again.

CHAPTER 3

I didn't know how long I had run or how deep I had gone into the jungle. I had been running scared, hollering, smashing into things, making a lot of noise.

I hadn't stopped to consider the attention I might be drawing to myself. I'd read an article by Dr. Ian Malcolm, a scientist who'd been to this island. He said raptors and other meat-eating predators lived on the island. But their usual prey knew enough to be quiet.

Not me.

I finally forced myself to slow down, catch my breath, and take in my surroundings.

I saw trees, vines, leaves, earth, and rocks. Thick jungle in every direction. I heard movement in the brush.

BRACHIOSAURUS

I didn't move. Maybe it was dinosaurs. Maybe not.

This wasn't just part of Jurassic Park, it was also an island near Costa Rica. Ben had said there were seventeen deadly snakes common in the jungles of Costa Rica. There were also tarantulas and bats and all sorts of other fun things waiting out there.

I heard movement again, but this time the sound was farther away. Whatever it had been was retreating. That was good, so long as *I* was the thing it was retreating from.

The bugs were biting, and I was starting to itch. Moths and butterflies fluttered nearby. Iguanas clung to branches. Frogs peeked out from leaves.

I was lost. I didn't have any idea how to get back to the shore or where I could go to find safety.

Then another thought hit me. How was anyone going to find me?

I remembered that in his article, Malcolm said Isla Sorna was "only" twenty-two square miles.

"It sounds like a lot," he wrote, "but considering the number of animals living on the island and the fact that they're multiplying, well, you do the math. Give it a few years, and the dinosaurs will be elbow to elbow."

Twenty-two square miles *did* sound like a lot. How could rescuers find one person—namely *me*—in all this?

I had to do something. I had to make sure they would know where to look for me.

I trudged on, and soon the light got more intense, like it did in late afternoon. The day was winding down and soon night would be coming. I had been hiking a long time. My stomach growled. I was incredibly thirsty.

Thump-thump-thump—

For only a couple of seconds, my exhaustion had overcome my fear. Now the fear was back. Some*thing* was coming, not some*one*, and it was probably coming for me. I looked for someplace to hide, but all I saw was the same thing everywhere: trees, vines, earth, rocks . . .

I looked up and saw the sun low and intense through the leaves.

Thump-thump-thump—

I heard a skittering. A shriek. Something small, maybe my size, was moving fast and heading my way!

I jumped and grabbed a heavy branch, then started climbing.

I got to the highest branch that could hold me and curled up, watching the ground below. I didn't see what had been running toward me. Either it had gone another way or it had run right past while I'd been climbing.

Thump-THUMP-THUMP—

The tree shook. Leaves fell onto my face, making me jump.

Then nothing. Whatever it was had stopped somewhere close. I couldn't go back down without risking running right into it.

I looked up. I wasn't high enough to see over the canopy of branches and get a sense of where I had ended up.

So I had a choice. Stay put in the trees, where it was safe, where whatever that big thing was couldn't get me, or take a risk and try to cover more ground. Maybe I'd find food and water. Maybe I'd get eaten.

I knew what my dad would do. I knew what Ben would do. I started thinking that my dad might have had his reasons for playing things safe.

A butterfly landed near my hand. It had black wings with yellow streaks that looked like bones and two little red dots that might have been burning eyes in the center of a skull. It was a Heliconia butterfly.

I didn't take its appearance as a good omen.

A sound came from below me and I tensed. Sprinting across a branch was a two-toed sloth. It moved so quickly it looked like it was surfing!

With only a slight hiss to mark its passing, it was gone.

The dinosaurs hadn't wiped out the island's animal population. If sloths lived here, then monkeys might, too. Whatever they ate, I could probably eat.

The skull-face butterfly sat nearby. Another sloth raced across the branch below.

I jumped down to the branch and followed it.

It's okay, Eric, said a voice in my head as I moved from tree to tree. *Just be careful. Be careful.*

The voice wasn't threatening or frightening or anything. It was just firm and familiar, and it made me feel better. It was Dad's voice.

Without leaving the safety of the trees, I was able to move across the jungle. Pretty soon I was far enough away from whatever had been making those thumps to start relaxing a little.

As the sun set, I caught up with the pair of sloths. Weird-looking things. Kind of a cross between a monkey and a possum.

The two sloths were chowing down on *bananas*. I stopped and really looked at the tree I had come to. It was a banana tree. Heavy bunches of bananas hung from its branches. I greedily snatched a couple of ripe ones and started eating with shaky hands.

In the past few weeks, Ben's platinum Visa

had allowed my mom and me to try expensive delicacies from three different countries. Not one tasted as good as this. Not one.

I stuffed myself, then curled up, thankful that some group of carnivores hadn't come along, thankful that it was just me and the sloths.

Night came and I got sleepy listening to a frog serenade.

I was still scared, but I told myself it was just a matter of time. Any hour, I expected to hear the whirring of helicopter blades and the sounds of people shouting into bullhorns.

Rescue would come. Surely my mom would send for help.

The night grew darker and I forced myself to stay awake, terrified that I'd be asleep and the rescuers would walk right by and never find me.

"They're coming," I whispered, hugging myself. "They *have* to come."

But what if, for whatever reason, it took another day, or another *couple* of days? Grant, Malcolm, all the others—they'd been rescued after a matter of *hours*, not days.

How was *I* supposed to survive? I didn't have any weapons or any supplies. I didn't know what I was doing. I didn't stand a chance!

A terrible thought struck me so hard that for a few seconds I could barely breathe.

Was *that* why they hadn't come? Did they think I was already dead?

"I'm here!" I screamed into the night. I heard my voice echo in the darkness. "Help me! I'm here! Please!"

I screamed until my throat was raw. But there was no answer that night. No sound of rescue. My voice simply joined the chilling chorus of grunts and squawks and eerie ancient cries that hadn't been heard on this earth for 65 million years.

Too exhausted to be afraid anymore, I curled up against the branches and finally closed my eyes.

CHAPTER 4

I woke up with a sore neck and an aching back. For just a couple of incredibly sweet seconds, I didn't remember where I was. I thought I was home, safe.

Then I remembered everything and the fear knotted up in my stomach all over again. Ben was dead, I was alone, and there were things that would kill me on sight pretty much everywhere.

Thinking about all that, I didn't have much of an appetite.

The rescuers will come for me.

I kept telling myself that over and over, as if thinking it were enough to make it true.

ANKYLOSAURUS

But . . . what if they didn't come *today?*

Something my dad used to say came to me: *Hope for the best, plan for the worst.*

I had to keep my strength up. I had to survive until the rescuers came. I had to be ready to go with them.

I felt weak, so I forced myself to eat a few more bananas.

I had to plan my day. Figure out a way to signal somebody (a passing motorboat, a low-flying plane, or the rescue helicopter) that I was here—without getting myself eaten by dinosaurs in the process.

Looking around, I saw that I was in a grove of banana trees. The neat, ordered rows gave the place the look of something planted by farmers. It was a mystery, but I had bigger things to worry about.

The sloths were sleeping. Snuggling, actually. The sight made me smile, despite how I was feeling.

"Hey, you guys," I said, shaking a branch. They lazily raised their heads. "Where's a good place to light a signal fire or something around here?"

I didn't like the idea of straying too far from this place. I had no idea if I'd find much of anything else that I could eat on the island. On the other hand, I couldn't just wait here and do nothing.

The sloths went back to sleep.

Well, it wasn't like I expected an answer or anything. Hearing my own voice and joking around made me feel a little less alone, that was all. Maybe a little less scared, too.

I tried climbing high enough to get a view of the outlying area, but I couldn't squeeze through the tight branches above.

Suddenly, the tree started shaking. I grabbed hold of a branch and shouted as a huge, dark head crashed through the tree's upper reaches. I fell, my arms outstretched, and grabbed at something hot and slippery. I hung on just long enough to surf downward along its slick surface a good ten or fifteen feet before I fell to the ground.

As I dropped like so much dead weight, I saw something brown and mushy below. A mud puddle? Then I crash-landed into it, sending mud—or whatever it was—flying everywhere.

When the smell hit me, I almost lost my breakfast. It was dino dung, and above me was a longneck tearing at the thick green foliage of the banana tree.

Oh, man! And I thought that other sauropod's gas attack was bad!

The ground shook as the dinosaur took a step closer. I looked around and saw that I was in a clearing on the other side of the banana tree grove. Three of the longneck's buddies were heading toward me. They were smaller than the one I had accidentally used as a water slide, but still big enough to trample me if I didn't move!

I stepped out of the dung that had broken my fall and made like I was on the track team. Finally, I slowed my sprint to a jog and looked back over my shoulder.

I couldn't get over those small oval heads on those incredibly long, lean necks running down into giant, football-shaped bodies. Their legs were elephant-like and their tails long, thin, and rigid, except for the tips, which swayed like serpents and coiled like whips.

The necks and tails of the dinosaurs stayed parallel to the ground as they walked, and between the largest one, a good eighty feet long, and the thirty- to fifty-foot-long "babies," I felt like I was watching a family of old-fashioned round-bellied vacuum cleaners with legs sauntering along.

I knew they weren't Brachiosaurus because they didn't have the deep, domed head. I'm pretty sure they were Diplodocus. The largest of them, Big Momma, had a neck that was close to twenty-five feet long, its body a dozen feet long, its tail a good forty feet long. Yeah, definitely dippies.

Incredible! I couldn't look away from them. I should have, though. The ground gave out under me, and suddenly I was tumbling down a steep slope. I rolled and banged my head and arms a dozen times on tree stumps and small stones. The world kept turning over while my stomach felt like it might come up through my mouth. I splashed into the warm water of a stream and came to a stop.

A pair of dinosaurs drank at the opposite side of the stream. They looked a little like rhinos, only they were twice the size of the animals I had seen on nature preserves and they didn't have horns on their triangular heads. Thick bands of armor with large plates and spikes wrapped around their bodies, and their thick, heavy tails ended in bony clubs that they waved menacingly as they looked up and glared at me.

Ankylosaurus. *Unhappy* Ankylosaurus.

I must have startled them. A little farther back, near a couple of trees, a pair of their young huddled.

I got up and put my hands up in front of me. "It's okay, it's okay!"

The angry clubtails watched me as I backed away. Then they stopped.

The biggest snake I'd ever seen hung from a

branch just a few feet over the head of the smaller of the two young Ankylosaurus. The snake's mouth was open, its fangs bared.

I didn't know if a snake could bite through the hide of a young dinosaur. What I *did* know was that if it could, and if the snake was poisonous, the little clubtail probably wouldn't survive.

I circled around the bigger Ankylosaurus and dipped my hand into the water. Fishing around, I came up with a nice-sized rock.

"Believe me, it's okay," I said. "I'm trying to help!"

Then I pulled my hand out of the water and threw the rock! It hit a branch near the snake, startling it and making it retreat from the Ankylosaurus young.

A home run!

The bigger Ankylosaurus didn't exactly see it that way. Both slammed their club-tails to the ground, kicking up rock and other debris. I stumbled back, but a big chunk of stone struck my right shoulder. It spun me around and I fell face-first into the water.

Scrambling, I tried to use my hands to push myself up out of the waist-deep water, but my right arm was numb. I got up, gasping for air, and heard the pair of angry Ankylosaurus storming into the water behind me.

Clutching my arm, I made it to the shore, then ran as fast as I could away from the dinosaurs. They didn't follow me very far. I guess they didn't want to leave their young unprotected. I made it to a bend in the stream and was soon out of sight of the dinosaurs.

I stood holding my hurt shoulder, panting from exhaustion.

I had only been trying to help!

Another saying of my dad's came to me: *No good deed goes unpunished.*

I used to think it was a stupid saying. But it seemed especially true now.

This was not a human—or humane—world. Whatever I did here, my good, *human* intentions could have consequences that I could not control—or even foresee.

I waded into the hip-deep water, splashing it on myself to wash off some of the dino dung. I crossed the stream and entered the shelter of more jungle. The feeling slowly returned to my arm.

CHAPTER 5

The next two days in the jungle, I mostly slept in the trees. I found fresh water to drink, and when I was just about to fall down from fear, hunger, and desperation, I managed to spear a fish.

The cooking fire I made with a lighter I carried turned out to be a bad idea. It drew what looked like an army of Compsognathus, chicken-sized meat-eaters, then something about the size of a human being. It moved so fast, and it was so dark, I couldn't tell what it was.

I was glad I could climb.

COMPSOGNATHUS

It was the only thing that saved me.

The third morning, I was pushing on, not really sure what direction I was going but still sure that a rescue party would come for me. I just had to hang on. Stay alive.

Finally, I moved aside the branch of a tree and saw the cracked windshield of an overturned Land Rover.

The first sign of civilization! I couldn't believe it!

I climbed around the overturned vehicle and nearly shouted with relief when I saw the parking lot and the vast main building of the InGen compound, which covered several acres.

I eagerly searched the skies, looking for rescue choppers.

Nothing.

I scanned the ground for any new tracks from all-terrain vehicles or human footprints.

Nothing again.

Cars and trucks had been upended and smashed in the parking lot. There were no recent dinosaur tracks. It looked as though the damage had been done a while ago.

I found a door at the rear of a building and saw scratch marks all around it. The knob turned easily, and I went inside.

I entered a dark corridor filled with empty

cages. Shattered high windows let in a dim golden glow.

I closed the door behind me. Locked it. It came to me then that any rescue parties would probably start their search here in the large main building of the compound. This was the most easily defended place I had found yet on Isla Sorna.

Right now, it felt like home, and I decided I was staying.

My stomach rumbled.

I foraged and came across a snack machine at the end of a vine-covered hall. I picked up a chair and was ready to smash the glass, but then I remembered I had picked up a couple of things from Eddie Campbell, a guy I had hung out with when things were at their worst with my parents.

I found a bottle opener in a desk and used it to work the lock and pop open the door. If this was home, there was no sense having broken glass all over the place. The same trick worked on the soda machines.

I wasn't going to starve here, that much was for sure.

In another room, I found the communications systems. Dinosaurs had been through the place. A lot of stuff was smashed up. Going through some of the lockers, I found some backup radios that hadn't been touched. All I needed was a way to power them up; then I could call for help!

The power was down all through the complex, but I figured there had to be emergency generators *somewhere*. It was just a question of finding them!

For the first time since Ben had died, I let myself feel a little happy.

I searched for the emergency generators for the rest of the day. Down one corridor, I stumbled upon some weird stuff. Places where they must have done some of their mad-scientist stuff. Genetic engineering. Making dinosaurs.

I found the building's lobby, too, off the computer lab. It was your typical high-ceilinged corporate lobby, and it had clearly once been very luxurious. But now the jungle was reclaiming it.

In the waiting area, the cushions of sofas and chairs had been gnawed at and pulled apart. The water in the cooler was black and swimming with gross-looking stuff. Moldy coffee mugs and ashtrays lay on the table. And roots and ivy poked through the floor and walls.

I spotted a phone on the reception desk, shrugged, and picked it up. Of course, the line was dead. And even if it had been live, it probably wouldn't have been an outside line.

A fluttering sound made me jump. I looked up and saw birds nesting in the rafters. The place gave me the creeps, so I left the lobby and continued my search. But I mostly found a bunch of locked rooms that I couldn't break into.

That night, I slept on a couch in one of the offices with barred windows. In the middle of the night, I felt something on my hand. A dull pressure. Something nipping, biting, nibbling. I woke and saw a rat sitting on my hand. I hollered, and it leaped off me and ran.

I locked the door and barricaded it.

When I finally got back to sleep, I dreamed that meat-eating compies had slipped through the bars on the windows and swarmed me. I only drifted in and out of sleep after that.

The next morning, I was really determined to find the emergency generators. I chose a new wing and began checking the rooms down one hallway. Most were offices. Records. Accounting. Personnel. Lots of storage.

Then, down a small corridor, I found them. There was a painted sign on the thick steel door to clue me in.

It was the one room that required an electronic keycard for access.

In other words, the only way you could get to the emergency generators if the power failed and the generators hadn't kicked on by themselves was with an electronic keycard that required power to read it!

I'm not going to repeat the things I started screaming. After I was done pounding and kicking and throwing things at the door, I started going office to office, hoping to find something that would help.

In one of the desks I found a ring of metal keys. In another office I found an empty backpack. In a maintenance closet I found tools—a hammer, a crowbar, screwdrivers, and a few cans of spray paint. I put everything I found into the backpack, then went back to the room that held the generators.

I tried to pry the thick steel door open with the crowbar, to pick the keycard lock with a screwdriver. But nothing worked. After smashing at the door with the crowbar until I was exhausted— I barely made more than a few small dents—I sprayed *DUH!* on it, then realized I should have sprayed it on myself. There might be a window!

I ran to the nearest office, climbed out its window, and jumped to the ground. I jogged alongside the building, but there was no window to the emergency generator room—just concrete blocks.

I pounded and kicked the blocks; then, exhausted, I went back to the snack machines, had something to eat, and started exploring more of the rooms. Maybe I'd find some other source of power for the radios.

Something ran through the hallway to my right. I gasped and nearly tripped as I backed into a chair. Then the thing came bounding toward me.

A sloth.

It leaped toward a window and was gone.

After that, I swore I'd always walk around with the crowbar in my hand. That or some kind of weapon.

That's my last nerve and you're on it, my mom said sometimes. For the first time in my life, I understood how she must have felt.

I used the keys I'd found to open more doors that led to more halls, more offices, and a couple of labs. I found a rec room with a Foosball table, a dartboard, a deck of cards, barbells, and free weights.

One locked door led to a vast food depot for dinosaurs, with processed soy patties for plant-eaters and a walk-in freezer filled with dripping red meat that had gone bad and wasn't really red anymore.

I grabbed one of the soy patties and tried it. Yuck. It tasted bland, like tofu, though it had a nutty smell.

After that, I took the spray paint cans and went to the roof. I nearly fell when I saw a Pteranodon circling in the far distance, so I worked fast.

Before the day was done, the words ERIC IS HERE were painted on the roof. When the choppers came, they would know right where to look.

Those first couple of days in the InGen compound, as tense as they were, hadn't been so bad because I had things to do.

In the days following, though, I had time to think. Way too much time. Even while using the rec room, I was still *thinking*.

I remembered times when my mom and dad were getting along. One fishing trip especially.

I thought about Ben. How much I missed him. How unreal it was that he was gone, that I'd never hear his voice again.

I wrote letters to my friend Jenn, telling her about this place.

I wondered where the rescuers were, and I refused to believe they weren't coming at all.

So I found things to do to keep myself busy. I read technical manuals and bound printouts. I dug into every desk and closet.

One morning, I solved the banana mystery.

There had been a small human population on Isla Sorna before the island had been bought by John Hammond—the man who'd created Jurassic Park. Most of the population had worked on several banana plantations throughout the island.

The plantations were now abandoned, but the banana trees had been left as a food source for the opossums, monkeys, and sloths living on the island. The printouts with that information also had a map of where to find the banana groves. I kept that and put it in my pocket.

I found a stream near the back of the compound, and I used it to take baths and wash my clothes. There was also a latrine—not something I want to talk about.

One day I got the idea to try to hot-wire a Land Rover the way I'd seen my old friend, Eddie, do with cars left overnight at the Westgate Shopping Center back in Oklahoma. I couldn't make anything happen. Either I was doing everything wrong, or the battery was dead, or both.

I got out of the Land Rover and buried my head in my hands.

"Well, Dad, you should be really proud of me," I said. "I'm playing it safe. Not going anywhere. Just a little crazy, maybe, but I'm not budging."

I looked to the sky, praying for some sign that rescue was coming.

Nothing.

A few days after that, I was so bored I *had* to go outside again. I turned the crowbar into a hockey stick and made goalposts out of two tree branches.

I used the dry soy patties as hockey pucks.

"All right, here he goes!" I hollered.

I ran forward and was about to swing my

hockey stick when I saw a raptor sitting on a rooftop less than a hundred yards away.

A *raptor*.

I froze.

It had been so long—so many days had passed and nothing had happened—that I'd started acting like nothing *would*.

Stupid, I thought. *I'm so stupid—*

The raptor hissed and leaped into the air!

CHAPTER 6

I didn't move as the raptor
landed on the hood of a
car. It took me a few
seconds to realize that
the animal wasn't looking
my way. Instead, it was
sniffing one of the candy
wrappers I'd left lying
around.

I didn't move as the raptor
landed on the hood of a
car. It took me a few
seconds to realize that
the animal wasn't looking
my way. Instead, it was
sniffing one of the candy
wrappers I'd left lying
around.

    I tried to remember
everything I'd learned
about Jurassic Park.
Dr. Grant's two
books, the one
by Ian Malcolm.
All the other di-
nosaur books I'd
read.

RAPTOR

    The raptor stood about
six feet tall, so at first I thought it was a
Deinonychus, the most common type of
raptor. But it had a long, low, flat snout,

like a crocodile, and its sickle claws were smaller than those of a Deinonychus.

It looked like a Velociraptor, but the Velociraptors that lived during the Age of Dinosaurs were about the size of a wolf. This one was the size of a grown man! This must have been what Dr. Grant and Dr. Malcolm meant when they talked about "genetically bred anomalies." These Velociraptors had been super-sized!

I tried to recall things I'd read about the behavior of dromaeosaurs, the family of dinosaurs that included Deinonychus and Velociraptor.

These animals had large brains and were considered to be pack hunters. That meant there might be other raptors around!

Suddenly, I heard a scrambling at my back and something launched itself at me—

I brought up the crowbar and tried to turn, but I wasn't fast enough. Something struck my back, sending me sprawling to the ground, the crowbar flying from my hand. I heard what must have been a dinosaur coming again. I tried to twist and turn, but it slammed down on my back, pinning me in place.

I couldn't believe this was happening. My mind wouldn't accept it—I was about to be ripped to pieces!

I opened my mouth to yell, but whatever was

sitting on my back shifted its weight, squeezing the air from my lungs.

I was going to die. I was going to be slashed open by raptors and eaten.

At the edge of my vision, I could see beneath the chassis of a dark green jeep. I heard a high yip and the crush of claws sinking into the earth.

The raptor that had been leaping from car to car was on the other side of the jeep. I saw its sickle claws spring forward from its feet and tap the ground.

The dinosaur holding me down was waiting for its friend, I thought. That's what was happening. It had to be!

Or—the two were competing for food and the raptor on my back wanted me all for itself.

The seconds moved slowly. My breath came back, but I stayed quiet. I was shaking, terrified, but there was nothing I could do.

I watched the raptor on the other side of the jeep kick around another candy wrapper. Then it moved off and I lost sight of it.

Sweat poured into my eyes. It stung. I heard soft footfalls but couldn't tell if they were coming closer or moving away. Labored breathing sounded above me.

The dinosaur that had knocked me down sounded *scared*.

Minutes went by. I didn't think, couldn't think. All I could do was wait to be slaughtered.

Then the pressure that had been on my back was gone. I looked for the crowbar, spotted it, and scrambled for it. I rolled, sprang to my feet, the weapon raised—

And saw a four-foot-high duck-billed dinosaur stuffing the processed soy hockey puck into his mouth. He stood on thick, round, three-toed hind limbs and had small forelimbs ending in hooflike claws with tiny little nubs that might one day develop into thumb spikes. His blubbery hippopotamus-like body was covered in gray- and brown-mottled scales and his heavy hindquarters ended in a short, tapered tail.

He was a juvenile Iguanodon. A herbivore. A plant-eater!

I didn't let go of the crowbar. I looked around, trying to spot any other threats. When I looked back, the Iguanodon was munching on one of my goalposts.

I spotted the candy wrappers that had drawn the raptor's attention and ran around the parking lot, grabbing them and stuffing them in my pocket. I'd find someplace to get rid of them later.

I'd been stupid. *Careless*.

My dad wouldn't have made a mistake like that. When we'd gone camping in the mountains together, he'd lectured me about not leaving any food around because it might attract bears. At the time, I thought he was just being Mr. Play-It-Safe. I even laughed about it with Mom later. I mean, we hadn't seen one bear the whole week we were camping!

Now I wish I could take that laughter back. Obviously, we hadn't seen a bear *because* we'd followed my dad's rules and hadn't left any food around!

I kept the Iguanodon in view as I backed up to the main building of the compound. My hand was still shaking as I opened the door. The Iguanodon was ignoring me, happy to chomp on the leaves of the branches I'd made into goalposts.

I stepped inside and closed and locked the door behind me. Then I found a small desk and dragged it over to the door to barricade it.

Standing on the desk, I could look out through the door's small upper window. The Iguanodon was outside, wandering around as if nothing had happened.

Maybe for *him,* nothing really had. Nothing unusual, anyway. A hungry predator had nearly come upon him, and so he had hidden.

But . . . he had also saved my life. After everything I had seen on the island, including the way the dinosaurs usually acted, this just didn't make sense.

I climbed down and spent the rest of the day sealing off and fortifying one section of the main building. I chose the hallway with the rec room and computer lab. There were candy, snack, and soda machines nearby, and sofas to sleep on. Many of the windows were barred, too, so I didn't have to worry about them. As for the other, shattered windows in that section, I broke down desks and chairs for wood and boarded the windows up as best I could.

It wasn't safe out there. I had done a stupid thing and I had nearly paid for it with my life. But I could learn.

I swore then that I wouldn't leave the main building of the compound until help arrived. I promised myself I wouldn't take any more risks, I wouldn't make any more mistakes.

More of my father's words came to me: *Don't make promises you can't keep.*

I would keep this one. I was certain.

My life depended on it.

CHAPTER 7

A crash woke me that night. At least, I thought it was a crash. A real sound, not something I had dreamed or imagined.

Being on the island, isolated, with no one to talk to for days and days, had made the line between things that were real and things that were imagined pretty thin. I felt jumpy and on edge.

I remembered dreaming of a rescue party. Soldiers wearing high-tech armor and carrying enough firepower to make sure we'd all get out alive. Like something out of a comic book or a movie. They kicked down doors and fried dinosaurs. They made a lot of noise.

I didn't go right away to check out the crash

IGUANODON

that woke me. I waited for a long time where it was safe. No other noises came, but my nerves wouldn't settle down.

I started thinking—what if a rescue party *did* come? Would they use bullhorns and spotlights and make the kind of noise that would attract dinosaurs?

It would make more sense to be quiet. Stealthy. To make noise only by accident. They were human. They could screw up, just like I had.

I started picturing rescuers going from room to room, not finding me, and taking off.

We better change that sign on the roof to ERIC WAS HERE, a rescuer would say. *Dinos must have got him.*

I got off the couch and quietly removed the barricades from the door. Then I strapped on a tool belt I'd loaded up with things I could use as weapons and went into the hall.

I didn't need the penlight I carried. The sun was rising, and an orange haze filtered in through the high, barred windows.

After passing a couple empty offices, I went through the rec room. I nearly stumbled over some free weights. I checked half a dozen closets.

Finally, I found what had made the noise. I shined my penlight on the floor of one of the offices with boarded windows. I saw books and paperweights. A bookshelf had collapsed.

"Sheez," I said.

"Grmmm-mrrrph?" a voice called.

"Yaaaah!" I yelled, falling back and shining my penlight. I scanned the dark room and saw scales and claws!

A deep growl sounded as my light struck black dinosaur eyes. A scaly arm swung out, and another crash came as books, printouts, and a globe smashed to the floor.

I had my back to the doorway. All I had to do was leap back and I could make it to the hall—but what if the dinosaur wasn't alone?

I risked a glance behind me and saw nothing. But I heard the dinosaur in the office rush my way. I reached for the door and tried to yank it closed, but the dinosaur was too fast for me. The door banged on its foot and a claw swiped at the air!

Jumping back, I dodged the claw and lost my balance. Falling, I snatched a heavy wrench from my tool belt and brought it around. Then I dropped onto my backside, my hand shaking, my breathing hard.

The dinosaur turned its back and started trashing the office for real. Within seconds, it reached the window and punched through the boards I had nailed in place!

Orange sunlight fell on the dinosaur, and I saw that it was the Iguanodon who had helped me avoid becoming raptor chow in the parking lot.

"What's going on, Iggy?" I asked. "What did I do, lock you in here with me?"

Iggy ignored me. He just continued thrashing about, hopping up and down, kicking wildly and kind of wobbling. An overturned container of quick-dry glue sat on the edge of the desk, and a puddle had formed on the floor. In its center was an inhuman footprint.

Stomp-stomp-crash!

Iggy had a *book* glued to his foot! He kept wobbling because he couldn't stand up right.

I laughed and started to relax. In a way, I was kind of grateful for the distraction. And I knew a way of making the dinosaur happy—*if* I could get him to go where I wanted.

The first thing I had to do was get that book off his foot. It was a paperback. I didn't recognize it. Not at first.

Then Iggy flopped to the floor and started kicking like a Rockette. I had to duck as the back cover stayed stuck on his foot and the rest of the book tore free and flew at me!

It hit the wall, and I looked away from Iggy long enough to see the name ALAN GRANT upside down.

Dr. Grant's book! The first one—the one he'd written before coming to Jurassic Park.

I put the wrench away and picked up the book. It made sense that many of the people working here would have had Dr. Grant's book on their shelves, but I was still surprised. It was one of my favorite books about dinosaurs.

I tucked the book into my waistband and looked back at Iggy, who had gotten over his tantrum and now looked like he was sulking.

For a second, I was tempted to go right up to him and lead him out of the room the way I might have with Gray, my dad's dog, but I had learned enough about dinosaurs to know that would be a bad idea. Just because Iggy was a plant-eater, and just because he saved my life once, didn't mean he wouldn't slam me into a wall or break half my ribs if I did something to tick him off. And we were both edgy enough as it was.

I had to do something about him, though.

It was a short trip to the food store. I brought back a couple of soy patties and left a trail of crumbs for Iggy to follow. Before I had gotten to the door of the storage room, Iggy was there, anxiously padding my way. I hugged the wall as he chuffed and raced into the room, attacking the food supply as if he were in heaven. Which I guess he was.

The sun was all the way up by the time I got Iggy squared away. All I wanted to do was stuff myself with junk food and sit down with Dr. Grant's book. It was the book that had gotten me seriously interested in dinosaurs in the first place—and it was one thing that I was pretty sure would take my mind off my situation.

I got breakfast and sat down in the rec room.

I hadn't read more than a couple pages when I saw I had almost tripped on those free weights because they'd been moved. *Iggy again,* I thought. I put the book in my waistband and shoved the weights back in place. As I put them back, I noticed that the edge of the rug had been clawed a little. I pulled at one corner and found a handle for a small hatch. The handle squeaked as I yanked on it with my right arm, which was still a little sore from what happened with the Ankylosaurus.

A little hideaway was revealed. It was mostly empty, but jammed into one corner was a pair of rollerblades with a tag that said CONFISCATED. I pulled out the blades and tried them on.

Eddie had a pair like this, and he used to let me practice with them. My dad wouldn't let me have my own—he said it was too dangerous.

Of course, my dad hadn't known half the stuff me and Eddie were doing, though my mom finally figured it out. Eddie went to juvie and said I had just been walking by that night we trashed Deputy Thompkins's car. My mom said it was one of the reasons I had to be taken out of Enid. Too much energy.

"Energy." Yeah, right. And my "energy" became just one more excuse for my parents to keep fighting.

Neither one of them had any idea why I was doing all that stuff. Maybe I didn't, either. But they were the adults. Shouldn't they have figured it out? Seen how angry I was?

But they didn't. They just didn't notice.

I stood up and stretched, yawning really loudly.

My yawn was met by a pair of growls. One from the right. The other from the left.

The room turned to ice.

I was finally being noticed.

A pair of raptors were in the rec room with me.

CHAPTER 8

The raptors leaped, and I pushed off with the blades. The rug made it hard to get the traction I needed, but I moved fast enough for the predators to hit each other instead of me.

I was scared, but this time, I didn't have the choice of waiting for the threat to disappear. I had to be fast. It was the only thing that mattered.

I grabbed at the first thing I saw: the free weights. I was almost at the door when I heard the raptors screeching and scrambling to their feet. I lobbed a

RAPTORS

free weight in the direction of the sounds. Another shriek came, and I was almost to the door. Then a rush of air, and a raptor was in front of me, blocking the way.

The blades gave me speed but messed up my ability to maneuver. I tried to pivot and toppled to one side. I was lucky that I was close to the wall. I grabbed a couple darts from the dartboard and lobbed them at the raptor. Two hit—one in the face, close to its eye. It flinched and moved from the door, nearly slamming into its buddy.

Nearly.

Now one raptor was distracted for a few seconds, but the other was coming right for me. I pushed off from the wall and dove as the raptor leaped. It went clean over me and hit the wall. I flopped onto the floor, half under the Foosball table.

The raptor I had tagged with the darts scrambled after me, and I kicked at it with the blades. It screeched and fell back. Then I brought my feet up, thrust them at one end of the Foosball table, and pushed with all my strength. It upended and fell onto the yipping predator.

I was on my knees as the other raptor got up to face me.

Yiiiieeeehhhh!

The second raptor was in pursuit. I didn't look

back. Doors blurred as I passed them. A hard turn came up. I grabbed at the wall and almost wiped out as I turned. Then I got my balance back and heard the raptors gaining.

I wasn't going to make it. They were going to get me before I could even figure out where to go!

I looked into one of the computer labs. I saw sunlight streaming in from the busted-open double doors leading to the main lobby. The rusty lock must have been too weak to hold against a good kick.

Now I knew how the dinosaurs had gotten into my fortified little camp—and I knew what that crash I'd heard had really been.

Veering into an office, I ground almost to a halt on the carpeting. The closest raptor squealed as it ran in after me. I snatched up a three-inch-thick computer report from the desk and raised it just in time to block a kick from the dinosaur. Its sickle claw tore through the first part of the printout—and got stuck! Its little arms sliced empty air as it fell down.

I threw a disconnected computer monitor at the next one, nailing it just as it came blindly through the door.

Snatching up another printout, just in case I could possibly pull off the same trick twice, I hopped and slogged my way to the door. Then

I was out of the carpeted room and back on a nice slick surface in the lobby. I raced toward the door as I heard the raptors closing in behind me.

I burst outside—and stumbled in the mud. It had drizzled the night before. I hadn't heard the rain.

I grabbed at the laces of my blades, which were like dead weights now. I had to get them off, but the raptors were coming and there was no time!

I had jammed a tile knife into my tool belt to use as a weapon. I cut through the laces and kicked at the first raptor to pounce on me. The loosened rollerblade slid off my foot and slammed the raptor in the face. I used the printouts as a shield when the other one pounced on me. Its razor claws flashed and shredded paper flew into the air like confetti. My heart was racing. I sliced at the raptor's side with the tile knife.

It yelped and backed off. Then I snatched up a rock and struck its head, stunning it. It fell as I wobbled to my feet and half ran, half hobbled toward the parking lot, one heavy rollerblade still weighing me down. I cut the laces and slipped out of it while I was moving. I grabbed the blade and held on to it.

But—where could I go?

I heard thunder and saw a shadow. Clouds

moved in front of the sun. I leaped over the hood of a car and fell on the other side. I scrambled and ran, tripping on a rock and landing behind an overturned jeep.

In the grass, in the mud, I saw a handle. I yanked on it without thinking. A door that had been covered over with earth came open only partially. I squeezed myself into the dark, cold space of a hideaway like the one I'd seen in the rec room and hauled the door shut behind me.

I shined the penlight around. I was in some kind of bunker. A really small one, probably meant for storage.

Outside, I heard the raptors howling and yipping.

I turned the penlight off and sat alone in the dark, shaking, trying not to even *breathe* too loudly.

The rain came soon after that. Over the downpour, the steady thumping of watery fingers on the hatch, and the rolling thunder, I couldn't hear the raptors.

They can open doors, I thought. Dr. Grant had said that in his second book. *They can open doors. . . .*

I held on to the inner handle of the hatch, yanking on it so hard I thought my arm would fall off.

It must have been hours before I let go.

"I shouldn't be here," I hissed, my chest heaving. I kicked at the wall. "I shouldn't be here!"

I freaked out, threw myself at the walls, punched at them until my knuckles were bloody.

"I shouldn't be here!" I yelled.

I attacked the walls, clawed at them. My brain was on fire! I fell to the floor, gripping my skull, coughing and spitting up what little was in my stomach as my guts burned and my ribs ached.

I drew myself up in the corner, hugging my knees, pleading with my mother, my father, the U.S. Army—every grown-up who was *supposed* to be there to protect me—to rescue me.

"Where are you, where are you, where are you . . . ?"

Every day and every night I'd been waiting, and now I saw clearly for the first time: They weren't coming. They had abandoned me. Everyone I trusted. Everyone I believed in. They'd all turned their backs on me!

I was going to spend the rest of my life on this island. The rest of my *very short* life, probably, because all it would take was one mistake and I would be dead.

I didn't know how I could live like this. I

didn't know how I could do it.

I kicked the door open. "Here I am, here I am! . . ."

I didn't know who I was talking to. The rescuers? The raptors? I was half out of my mind.

The only thing that brought me back from the edge of losing it completely was a shaft of sunlight that shone on Dr. Grant's book. The book had fallen open to a certain page. With trembling hands, I took the book and stared at the passage glimmering in the light.

Many scientists believe the dinosaurs never really died out 65 million years ago, Dr. Grant had written. *These scientists believe dinosaurs live on today—as birds. The dinosaurs were too big and the food supply too small, so the dinosaurs became a likely example of natural selection—in short, they were forced to adapt or perish.*

I closed the book, then settled back and pulled the door shut. I sat in darkness. In silence.

Adapt or perish.

From the moment I crash-landed on this island, I had truly believed someone would come to rescue me. I was wrong. No one was coming. I was dead to the world outside Isla Sorna.

Now I had a choice. I could try to adapt. Try to

change my ways.

Or I could perish.

My dad told me to play it safe. He made me promise I'd be careful. I'd broken that promise. Sometimes I'd paid the price for breaking that promise. But at other times, not playing it safe was what kept me alive.

So what was I supposed to do? How was I supposed to change?

After what felt like several more hours, I turned on my penlight and looked at the printouts I had taken with me.

Most of it was boring, meaningless stuff—technical data, projections, construction reports. But it made the time pass and it kept my mind off how hungry I was—and how eventually I'd have to go back out there to get food.

Just like Iggy.

It wasn't until those long hours of waiting—of listening to the hammering rain, the thunder; of waiting for scratches and scrapes at the hatch, my nerves constantly jumping—it wasn't until then that I thought about Iggy. He had saved my life and I had left him behind. I hadn't led the raptors outside to draw them away from him. I had been thinking about my own survival. Nothing else.

I didn't want to think about that. I went back to my reading, but it was hard to concentrate.

Iggy had probably only saved my life that day because he was worried I'd do something to endanger his. It wasn't like I owed him anything. He wasn't human. The concept didn't apply, as my old biology teacher used to say.

It just doesn't apply, I repeated to myself.

I kept turning pages. Two pages stuck together. I flipped past them and was going to ignore them completely, but it kept bugging me, so I went back and peeled them apart. Someone had dropped mustard or something on them.

The first time I read those partially torn pages, I didn't exactly get what was on them. It took about three tries before I understood and believed what I was looking at.

They were plans for safe houses to be installed across the island. Rooms that were hidden away, where human beings could go if anything went wrong while dinosaurs were being transported. The rooms were to be loaded up with independent power supplies, weapons, food, and communications equipment.

Only one safe house had been approved and constructed as a test site.

I sat back and thought about it.

No one believed I was still alive. If I could find this place, if I could reach it and get inside, I could call for help. I could get home.

But it was a risk.

And the very idea of going out into that jungle terrified me.

I didn't even know *where* to begin searching.

"You'll never make it," I whispered to myself in the dank darkness.

But what else could I do? Stay here and hope?

Waiting and wishing and hoping. That's all I'd *been* doing. I had to act on this chance. I knew it. I had to adapt or perish.

But how was I going to do it? How would I even *find* it?

Staring at the edge of the torn page, I found my answer.

The page held a map to the safe house.

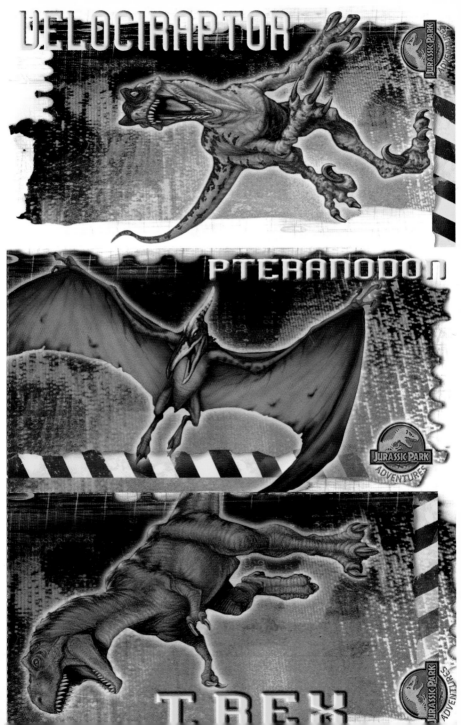

VELOCIRAPTOR

PTERANODON

T. REX

JURASSIC PARK ADVENTURES

Velociraptor

(vuh-LOS-ih-RAP-tur)
Carnivore (meat-eater)
Length: 6 feet (1.8 m)
Height: 6 feet (1.8 m)
Weight: 220 pounds (100 kg)
When: 85–75 million years ago
Beware of: Razor-sharp sickle claws!

DANGER!

Do not approach. One of the smartest and fiercest dinosaurs in Jurassic Park. Hunts in packs. Related to Deinonychus and Utahraptor.
NOTE: InGen's Velociraptors were bred larger than their ancestors, who were only about the size of a jackal—33 pounds (15 kg) and 1 foot high at the hips.

Pteranodon

(tuh-RAN-uh-don)
Carnivore (meat-eater)
Wingspan: 23–30 feet (8–10 m)
Size: 6 feet (1.8 m)
Weight: 55 pounds (25 kg)
When: 85–75 million years ago
Beware of: Attacks from above!

DANGER!

Among the largest flying creatures in Earth's history, Pteranodons have slender, toothless beaks and feed on fish.
NOTE: The Pteranodons of old did not have the strength to lift a human. But the genetic giants of Jurassic Park (up to 180 pounds with wingspans of 45 feet) are capable of carrying off human-size prey. Keep one eye on the sky!

Tyrannosaurus rex

(tye-RAN-uh-SAWR-us recks)
Carnivore (meat-eater)
Length: 40 feet (12 m)
Height: 13 feet (3.9 m) at hips
Weight: 7 tons
When: 70–65 million years ago
Beware of: Banana-sized teeth!

DANGER!

Do not approach. Powerful bite with very thick teeth, capable of crushing bone. Can swallow a small human in one gulp. Can run up to 25 miles per hour.

IGUANODON

ANKYLOSAURUS

BRACHIOSAURUS

Iguanodon

(ih-GWAHN-uh-don)
Herbivore (plant-eater)
Length: 35 feet (11 m)
Height: 9 feet (3 m) at hips
Weight: 5 tons
When: 135–120 million years ago
Beware of: Thumb spikes!

CAUTION!

Although plant-eaters, Iguanodons are not without defenses. Beware of the thumb spikes at the ends of their massive arms. These spikes are the perfect weapons for putting out the eyes of enemies!

Ankylosaurus

(ANG-ki-lo-SAWR-us)
Herbivore (plant-eater)
Length: 25 feet (7.5 m)
Height: 4 feet (1.2 m) at hips
Weight: 3 tons
When: 66 million years ago
Beware of: Club tail!

CAUTION!

These "tank" dinosaurs are well armored. Keep a respectful distance from their massive 3-ton bodies and the heavy bone clubs on their tails. NOTE: When swung from side to side, these clubs are at the same level as the knees of predators like Tyrannosaurus!

Brachiosaurus

(BRAK-ee-o-SAWR-us)
Herbivore (plant-eater)
Length: 80 feet (24 m)
Height: 50 feet (15 m)
Weight: 30 tons
When: 150 million years ago
Beware of: Being stepped on!

CAUTION!

One of the tallest dinosaurs that ever lived. Feeds on the leaves of trees. Don't miss a chance to look at this spectacular dinosaur, but steer clear of its massive feet!

CHAPTER 9

I read a book one time about a guy who gets put in jail for something he didn't do. He has to spend a week in solitary confinement.

No light.

No sound.

No one to talk to.

Nothing to do.

That's what it was like for the next few days in

TRICERATOPS

the underground hideaway outside the complex. The only difference was I didn't have a lock on my door. I could go out any time I wanted.

I could also get eaten by dinosaurs. Or trampled. Or crushed.

I'd read Dr. Grant's book three times. I had two maps, one telling me where to find banana groves, the other how to reach the safe house. All I had to do was get ready for the journey. No biggie.

Sure.

My face was flushed. It was hot and stuffy and I was sweating. I stank from caked-on mud and muck. I was shaking and feeling sick because that's what happened to me every time I thought about the miles separating me from the safe house and everything I might run up against between here and there.

I wasn't sure how many runs I'd made to the complex to gather food and supplies. Every one had been terrifying. I knew that no matter how cautious I was, something could always spring out of the darkness and surprise me.

I couldn't live like this. I wasn't sure I *was* living. Just *existing*.

It was an unusually cool morning when I decided to go for it. I had all my supplies with me. I was as ready as I was going to be.

I shoved the door open just wide enough so that I could put my hand through the opening and use the little mirror I'd found to check and see if any dinosaurs were around. I drew it back quickly, took a deep breath, and threw the door open.

I squeezed through the opening and went outside. I made it to the tree line and the fear hit me again.

No, not today. Tomorrow. Today, I was going back where it was safe.

This had been the third false start. I wasn't proud of myself. I kept thinking Ben would be calling me a wuss right now, while my dad would say I was being a smart and cautious young man.

Movement caught my attention. One of the big, squat cars in the parking lot, what I'd thought was a green jeep, started moving. Lumbering. I squinted and saw its horns.

A Triceratops. The dinosaur sniffed and chuffed, heading right for the hatch over my underground hideaway. I couldn't understand what it wanted. Then I saw the bold shaft of sunlight striking the hatch. With a snort, the Triceratops plopped down on top of the hatch and rested there. The dinosaur's head lolled and it went to sleep.

I didn't know how long it planned to sleep, but I kept thinking, *If I had been inside . . .* There were small cracks in the seal between the door and its frame. That's what let air in. The Triceratops was blocking those cracks with its two-ton body. If I had stayed in the hideaway, I either would have had to find a way to make the Triceratops move—

Or I would have suffocated.

Trying to get the Triceratops to move off would be dangerous. What was I going to do, poke it with a sharp stick, then act surprised when it tried to gore or crush me?

Now it was a risk no matter what I did. Every choice led to danger.

I turned and went into the jungle.

CHAPTER 10

Not far from the compound, I found a derelict water tanker resting headlight-deep in a swampy pond. I stopped to check it out, hoping there would be some communications equipment, but I couldn't find any. There was a small hold I could use as another hiding place, but I was done hiding. I moved on.

A couple hours into my journey, I tripped over a dinosaur's tail. I thought I was being so cautious. So slick. I was even starting to feel a little confidence. Until this.

TYRANNOSAURUS REX

The dinosaur was a rex, lying on its side.

I froze as I saw its head angle in my direction. No sudden movements. No movement at all. That was all that could save me.

The rex sniffed.

A low growl rose from the dinosaur's throat as its reddish brown flank trembled and one of its hands moved in my direction.

It smelled me.

I bolted. I got a good ten feet before my foot caught on a root and I fell and hit my head on a rock. It hurt and I was a little dazed, but I knew I was in danger and I couldn't stop.

I chanced a look back as I got to my feet, expecting to see the rex's maw open, expecting to smell its horrible breath.

The dinosaur was still lying on the ground, its tail slowly sweeping back and forth.

I looked around, confused. For whatever reason, the rex wasn't coming after me. That was all I needed to know. I turned to get back on the trail to the safe house when I heard movement from the trees ahead.

I couldn't see anything. The noise I heard might have been made by a couple of harmless sloths or monkeys. Only I was nowhere near any of the banana groves.

The sound came again. Louder this time. A rustle of low-lying tree branches and leaves. Whatever was making the sound was coming closer.

I backed up until I felt the rex's tail tap my shoes. I jumped and whirled.

The rex sneezed.

Suddenly, I heard sounds from every direction. Things were coming fast from all sides.

There was nowhere to go. I could see green-and-yellow scales about to burst from the jungle. Flashing claws. I heard hisses and inhuman screams.

If I ran to a tree and tried to climb, I'd be heading right for the predators.

I spotted a heavy branch a few feet over the top of the rex's head. I ran toward the rex and leaped onto the dinosaur's side. The rex's mouth opened wide and its head snapped forward. But I was already in flight.

With one leap, I went over the rex's head and planted my foot on the top of its skull. I bounded up, grabbed the branch, and swung my legs up high, wrapping them around the branch as I heard the rex bite at the air beneath me.

I heard a terrible ripping sound, and heard the rex bellow in pain. Looking down, I saw the animal surrounded by raptors.

The rex tried to defend itself, but it was too weak. I didn't know if it was sick or starving, but right now, it was prey.

The branch above me cracked and started to splinter. I shinnied across it, and found another handhold just as it snapped and fell toward the battling dinosaurs below.

A raptor climbed up on the rex, just as I had, and tried to leap at my dangling legs.

The rex caught the animal in its maw and chomped down. Two more raptors went for its neck.

I looked for healthy branches and carefully but quickly made my way across them. I went from tree to tree, the growls, howls, and shrieks of the war being waged behind me dwindling as the minutes stretched on.

My legs got so tired they felt like they were going to buckle, and I nearly lost my balance twice, so I stopped to rest. I scanned the ground below, worried that one of the raptors might have followed me.

All clear.

Okay.

I had to concentrate on moving forward. On getting to the safe house and radioing for help. So I did.

I stayed in the trees for two more hours, but it was slow going. I stopped long enough for a snack from my backpack and some water I'd bottled.

Checking below me one more time and seeing nothing, I was about to go back to the ground when I heard a familiar scratching and hissing. I froze, the fear hitting me before I even saw what I knew was making those sounds.

A trio of raptors appeared from inside a cluster of bushes below. Their green-and-black scales perfectly camouflaged them against the jungle leaves. Almost invisible.

That's what I wanted to be. Invisible. Undetectable. Every sharp, shuddering breath I took sounded to my ears like it had been aimed into a bullhorn. All the dinosaurs had to do was hear something, smell something, and look up—

They sniffed and closed on the base of the tree.

My hands were shaking as I held on to the branches and prayed they wouldn't make a sound. My head felt light, and my feet felt like they might slip and let me fall right in front of the predators.

I thought of nights Eddie and I spent watching houses in towns close to Enid. It was like this weird commando game we played, watching a family, getting to know when they'd be home, when they'd go out.

It wasn't until later that I found out why Eddie was really watching those houses. He sold the information to thieves, who broke in when no one was home.

The whole time we were watching a house, we had to be invisible. We had to camouflage ourselves any way we could. We'd spray-paint old blankets and cover ourselves with them to blend in with a garage wall or some darkened bushes.

If the raptors looked up now for any reason, they would see me. I had no camouflage. No cover.

The dinosaurs below took a whiff of a puddle near the roots, shrieked, and looked around fearfully. With high yips, they ran away in a blur.

I waited in the trees for a very long time, feeling my heart racing, making sure the predators had left. Climbing down, I went to the puddle and sniffed it.

"Aw, gross," I muttered. I recognized the smell. It was a scent I had picked up near the helpless rex. Tyrannosaur urine.

Raptors normally wouldn't mess with a healthy rex. If they thought a rex had just relieved himself in a spot, they worried that the rex was still nearby. Something they didn't want to deal with.

If I'd had a container, I'd have taken some of the urine with me.

Hours went by, and I found myself thinking about the rex. How had it gotten so deep into the jungle? Had it chased prey here, then gotten lost? Its size would have made it hard to sneak up on prey or to maneuver around the way it could in the outer reaches of the island.

I didn't know. It wasn't my problem. The only thing that mattered was surviving. Worrying about the problems of predators wasn't going to help me with that.

Or would it?

I kept walking and left the jungle. I reached a valley that had been completely deforested. The greens had been picked clean. Dr. Grant wrote about the way sauropods pretty much destroyed an area, then moved on. That's why so many sauropods from North America were later found in South America. They ate until North America was barren and had to keep moving south to find food. Dr. Grant said a lot of scientists think it's one of the reasons the dinosaurs really died out. No asteroid. They just ate themselves out of existence.

Fine. No greens meant no plant-eaters. No plant-eaters meant no food for the meat-eaters.

Still, I didn't feel safe. It was too open. If some raging predators were scouting the area, there were very few places to hide.

Cawwwwhrrr!

A Pteranodon sailed above. I thought of the one that had flown low, trying to catch the jumping fish, then me. Was it the same one? I found a couple of tree stumps and knelt between them, remaining still until the flyer was gone.

It was almost night when I left the valley and found a clump of old, withered trees. I chose a garlic tree that was ten feet around and pushed myself into a cleft in its trunk. There was enough light from outside for me to see that nothing else had picked this as a hiding place.

I went back out and fell into a mud puddle. I spat and cursed, then realized the stink of the mud would help to disguise my scent. I gathered broken branches, vines, and leaves, and hauled them inside.

Covering the opening with branches helped to further conceal my scent and gave me kind of an early warning system. I had to sleep. No choice. I figured if something knocked the branches down trying to get in, the noise would wake me.

I had the crowbar in a harness on my back. I still wore the tool belt filled with makeshift weapons.

Twice today I'd nearly been spotted by predators because I didn't blend in with my surroundings. I set a vine loosely around my neck, measuring the length I would need, then tied off a kind of necklace. From there I made ribbings with the vines that went down three feet in every direction. Then I attached leaves. When I was done, I had a poncho of leaves that fit neatly over my head. In the morning when I set off again, I'd blend in.

I settled down inside the massive tree trunk and slept lightly.

In the middle of the night, I thought I heard scratching sounds. I got up and checked the "door," but the branches hadn't been touched. Weird.

In the morning, I ate breakfast in the semi-darkness and prepared to go outside.

This was the moment I had grown to hate. Opening a door, never knowing if some dinosaur might be right outside. It had never happened. I didn't really think it ever would. But I knew all it would take was one really good mistake and I'd be dead.

I pulled one branch from the door, took out my crowbar, and slipped my little mirror outside with my free hand. I moved it to the left. Nothing. To the right—

A blur raced toward the mirror.

"Yiaaghh!" I screamed as something ripped across my hand, and I heard the mirror drop to the ground and shatter.

I stumbled back as the branches exploded inward and a raptor barreled right at me.

CHAPTER 11

I swung blindly with the crowbar and heard it connect!

The dinosaur hissed and dropped on its side as a couple of its teeth flew from its skull. I fell and snatched my pack. As the raptor came around for another attack, I yanked out a high-intensity flashlight and shone it in its face. It screeched and backed away from the blinding light within the darkness of the huge hollow tree trunk.

I hit it with the crowbar again.

I was afraid.

I was crazed.

I was as close to being an animal as I'd ever been.

As I hit the hissing dinosaur, I

STEGOSAURUS

heard even higher-pitched shrieks from above. I chanced a look upward and saw that the higher reaches of the hollow tree were filled with bats!

A blanket of bats descended on us. The light upset them—and kept them away from me. The raptor wasn't so lucky. They covered it and I took advantage. I grabbed my pack and ran.

I scanned the grove and saw no other predators. The trees were spaced too far apart for me to climb and go from branch to branch, so I ran as fast as I could.

After the grove, I crossed a series of hills. In the distance, I heard the rush of water. My legs were ready to give out from under me when I got to the top of another hill and spotted a waterfall in the distance.

I looked back and didn't see anything following me, so I took out my maps and checked them. My fingers trembled with excitement as I traced the lines on the map and found the waterfall.

I was only three miles from the safe house.

In as little as an hour, I would be radioing for help.

By tonight, I would be going home!

It took twenty minutes to reach the waterfall. A couple of spike-backed Stegosaurus were keeping themselves cool in the shade of the falls. I didn't go anywhere near them. I didn't even make eye contact.

They ignored me, too.

The land was getting lush again, and I had found prey.

What *predators* would consider prey, I mean.

The ground to the west was mottled. Patches of green and brown were everywhere I looked. It must have been a feeding ground for plant-eaters.

I dunked my head beneath the waterfall and closed my eyes, but only for a second.

Then I headed out for the last leg of my journey. I went through a deep forest. The map showed a shorter route, but this way felt safer.

Pretty soon there were fewer trees, and the leaves above were thinning out. According to the map, the forest ended near the edge of the valley where the safe house had been built.

I heard sounds. Scratching. Snorting. A few growls.

As quietly as I could, I climbed the nearest tree and scaled along its sturdiest branch. The valley came into view, and relief flooded through me.

I saw dozens of Iguanodons in the bowl-shaped valley below. A huge herd. They wandered about, their heads low. Some were grazing.

I thought about Iggy and hoped he was down there with them.

Okay. I'd been cautious—as cautious as I could. I'd played by my dad's rules and it had paid off. Now it was time for my reward.

I went down a couple of branches and was about to leap to the earth below when a shadow stretched out across the ground below me. I waited, and a figure came into view, followed by three others.

Raptors.

I looked back to the valley and saw other figures standing near the edges to the east and the west. Then I climbed high enough to get a better look.

This valley wasn't a lush, green place. Not somewhere plant-eaters would stay for long—unless they didn't have a choice.

The Iguanodons were huddling. Some were looking to the ridges where the raptors gathered. I saw looks of what might have been fear and defiance. The full-grown Iguanodons were the size of rexes. They all had lots of meat on their bones.

They also had huge spikes on their hands. Paintings of Iguanodons and superpredators wrestling and fighting to the death came to my mind.

I had read about predators swarming herds. I knew what was coming.

A war was about to be fought.

My best chance of getting off the island lay right in the middle of what was about to be a battlefield.

CHAPTER 12

The raptors poured down into the valley and surrounded the Iguanodons. I watched for several long, tense moments as the predators circled the herd, looking for weakness.

They found it. A smaller Iguanodon slipped out from between two bigger dinosaurs and stumbled on the large tree stump marking the entrance to the safe house. The raptors, led by a large raptor with red rings on its chest and back, rushed toward the vulnerable young dinosaur.

RAPTORS

The Iguanodon's foot kicked up as he tried to right himself, and something bright and shiny caught the afternoon light.

The back cover of a book was glued to his foot.

It was Iggy.

I leaned forward, my muscles coiled, my body ready to spring. But—there was nothing I could do. Nothing except get myself killed right alongside Iggy.

They're dinosaurs, I thought. *I'm not a part of this.*

I gripped the crowbar. Iggy had saved my life.

But there were so many raptors. . . .

Suddenly, a larger Iguanodon broke from the herd and got between the terrified, stumbling Iggy and the oncoming tide of predators. It wasn't full-grown. It may have been Iggy's older brother or a friend.

Just like Ben had been my friend.

Two of the raptors leaped onto the bigger Iguanodon. It growled as their claws bit into it, and turned swiftly to shake them loose. Its thumb spikes smashed the flank of a third raptor that came at it; then it was overwhelmed. It fell as a dozen raptors attacked, led by the alpha male.

Iggy was on his feet now, his back to the other raptors. I expected at least a few of them to attack before he made it back to the safety of the herd. Instead, the raptors formed a defensive line, cutting the herd off from the dino they were savaging.

The Iguanodons closed ranks around Iggy. He looked back and yelped as he saw the raptors swarming the bigger dinosaur.

Then there was nothing but silence as the raptors fed.

I waited for the raptors to attack the rest of the herd. It didn't happen.

Night came and the stars appeared. The raptors went back to their positions above the valley. The Iguanodons huddled together, none of them looking in the direction of the predator's kill.

A soft rain fell. I heard a gentle moan. It might have been Iggy mourning for his lost friend, or it might have been the fast-rising wind. I didn't know.

I knew what my dad would tell me to do. *Wait it out in this tree and go down there into the valley when it's safe. You don't belong here, and you're not a part of this. Not even a little.*

I didn't know if I could wait it out. Maybe what I'd seen was just a warm-up for the big battle I'd expected. Or maybe something else was going on.

Lightning streaked across the sky. Thunder rolled. The raptors were startled.

The rain became heavier, and I jumped as

lightning struck a tree on the other side of the valley. The upper branches sizzled and fell. Nearby, the raptors scattered, shrieking and yipping.

Then I realized: To reach the valley, I was going to need a distraction.

I looked at the crowbar and pictured my dad putting a lightning rod on our roof.

You can never be too careful, he'd said.

I checked out the other trees. Many were taller than the one I was in. Still, I was at risk just holding on to the crowbar.

On the ground, about a dozen raptors seemed to be patrolling my side of the valley.

I made my decision.

Climbing to the top of the tree, I put the crowbar back in its "scabbard" on my back and gathered up some vines. The branches here were thinner and more brittle. One crackled beneath me, and I barely got off it in time. I heard it crashing to the ground and looked down to see if any of the raptors had heard it.

None of them came my way.

With trembling hands, I tied the crowbar to the treetop. The rain was chilling. Lightning flashed again. I froze with my hands on the crowbar, certain I would be electrocuted.

The lightning arced across the sky, but didn't connect with my tree.

I tied the bar as tightly as I could, then climbed down to the lower branches and quietly stole across to a branch from the tree to my left. If the tree with the crowbar *was* hit, I definitely didn't want to be in it at the time.

I hooked some rope from my pack around a heavy branch and started tying it in place. If I got lucky and the lightning went for the crowbar, I had to be able to get to the ground fast.

My hands were fumbling with the rope. I heard scuffing sounds and scratching from below. Had the raptors scented me?

I had to move faster, I—

Lightning zigzagged down from the sky. A blinding explosion tore into the tree to my right, sparks flying, leaves and branches instantly bursting into flame. Below, shrieks, squeals, and yips tore through the night.

I wasn't ready. The rope wasn't secure!

I heard what sounded like the breaking of a giant's back and turned to see the entire upper half of the burning tree to my right falling toward me!

There wasn't time to brace myself or to think about what I should do. My instincts told me to jump, and so I did. The trees smashed together behind me, and I felt flames sear my leg. Splintered branches snapped off and whipped against me as I fell. I was thrust forward, out over the edge of the valley. The ground raced up and I hit hard, hurting my shoulder and knee. I slammed into the slope of the valley, and the world spun over and over as I tumbled downward.

A figure rose up. Half turned my way.

I was rolling end over end like a bowling ball, and I struck the thing ahead like I was picking up a spare. It yelped and I mashed its head down against a rock and kept tumbling until my momentum slowed and I sprawled to a stop, the world spinning. I felt sick and my body ached.

I got to one knee as the valley swayed like a ship on rough waters.

I'd knocked down a raptor—and it was already getting back up.

I looked over my shoulder and saw that a hundred yards separated me from the Iguanodons and the hatch leading to the safe house.

Off to my right, I saw several cavities in the rock wall. Tunnels? Caves?

I heard the raptors hissing and shrieking. They made weird resonating sounds, unlike any I'd ever heard before.

The raptor I'd taken down wasn't looking my way. Not yet. Another flash of lightning and crack of thunder distracted it.

I had raced raptors before, but I didn't think I

could manage it this time. My head was throbbing and my legs were shaky.

I scrambled for the closest cave mouth, praying I wouldn't be spotted, praying I wouldn't find more predators inside taking shelter from the storm.

CHAPTER 13

The cave was deep and empty, as far as I could tell. I found a little niche and collapsed inside. I sat alone in the dark, shaking and waiting for the fear to pass. The storm got even worse outside. I was freezing sitting around in wet clothes. I'd lost my best weapon getting this far, and I was only halfway to the safe house.

I told myself I'd just rest my eyes. I couldn't go to sleep there. That would be crazy.

RAPTOR

I'm not sure when I woke up, but it was still dark. The storm was winding down.

I jolted awake, gasping. The moan I had heard earlier was still sounding. I didn't think it was the wind anymore. I knew that sound. I think I had been making it when I was standing there looking into Ben's eyes. They were open, but he didn't see me.

You've got to stay focused, I told myself.

I sat there and just listened for a while. If raptors had entered the cave while I was sleeping and hadn't noticed me, I didn't want to give them a reason to now.

I listened until I couldn't stand it anymore, then got up and explored the caves. I had a pocket flashlight, and I covered the beam with my hand so it would just give off a slight glow.

The caves were like a maze. I spent hours making sure I was alone and getting the layout down. It reminded me of the compound and made me think of all the things I could have done to set traps there and make the place more secure.

After I was done, I went to the mouth of the cave and looked out.

A small group of raptors sat nearby. Two were sleeping. The other three were picking some bones clean.

I cautiously backed up until I was deep inside the cave again. I swore under my breath.

I had to get down to the safe house, but the raptors stood between me and the hatch in the ground that served as the door.

It took me a while to come up with a plan.

Even longer to get the nerve to try it. But at last, I was ready.

I went back to the cave mouth, peeled open a candy bar, and left it sitting there. Then I went back into the maze.

I don't know how long it took. But eventually I heard them. The smell of the candy drew them, just like it had at the complex. They followed the trail of wrappers and treats that I had left. It led them to a fork and sent them scurrying down the tunnel to the left, where I had left another flashlight burning. Its batteries were wearing down, but the light was enough.

I was waiting behind a wall to the right, peering around the corner. My heart was racing as I counted all five. Once I saw the last of their tails going down the left-hand tunnel, I turned and quietly followed the curve of the walls until I came out near another cave mouth. I looked out and saw that the way down to the safe house hatch was now clear. Most of the Iguanodons in the valley were sleeping. A few were grazing on the small patches of greens left there.

I was about to take a step out when a raptor walked by. I froze and prayed it wouldn't smell me. I had covered myself in dirt from the cave to disguise my scent and the candy scent that had been on me from the bars.

It didn't stop.

I relaxed, took a step forward—and heard a scratching and a hiss from behind. I turned in time to see a raptor leap at me. Shuddering, I sidestepped and it missed me, its claws making a chilly breeze as they struck at the air near my face.

I had a rock in my hands and struck the raptor, stunning it before it could get up again, before it could make a sound.

I wondered for a second if this had been one of the raptors that had tried to kill Iggy. One of the predators that savaged Iggy's friend.

A part of me hoped so. I hit it again, then dropped the stone and made a run for the hatch.

CHAPTER 14

It was the longest hundred yards I'd ever run.

I was panting, my chest heaving. I tried to look in front of me, to the sides, even behind me as I ran. It was a miracle I didn't stumble.

The Iguanodons turned to look at me, several rising at the sound of the rocks I kicked with my every step. I saw Iggy move my way. He was near the hatch. Two bigger Iguanodons moved in front of him, one of them stepping right on the handle I'd need to pull.

Several rose up on their hind legs, brandishing their spikes.

I panicked. And I had panicked *them*.

Now I didn't know what to do. The Iguanodons were growling. Behind me, the raptors on the hill were yipping and heading toward me.

IGUANODON

I stopped. In the darkness, and with the way I was running, I could have been mistaken for a raptor by the Iguanodons. I'd scared them. Now I had to do something to show them I wasn't going to hurt them.

I stood still, hearing the raptors come up behind me. The Iguanodons were still twenty feet away. They could cover that distance with a few steps. Close ranks around me the way they had with Iggy.

They didn't.

I turned and saw one raptor ahead of a dozen more.

I heard movement from the Iguanodons.

They were stepping back.

I crouched and grabbed the first couple of rocks I could find. I lobbed one at the advancing raptor. The rock connected with a sharp crack and knocked the predator on its side.

Others were still coming.

I turned and ran. I raced over the hatch. There was no chance I could stop, crouch, and haul it open before the raptors reached me. None.

I ran for the herd. The Iguanodons growled and stamped their feet, but I wove my way between them. I darted to keep from being kicked or pounded or run through by one of their spikes.

The raptors hadn't followed.

I tripped and an Iguanodon's foot came down near my head. I got to my feet and grunted as a tail swept forward and struck my back, knocking me facedown. I rolled and avoided two more thunderous footfalls. My head hit a rock, and pain tore through me. For a couple of seconds, I was disoriented.

A couple of seconds was all it would have taken for the Iguanodons to finish me off. One good kick, a punch with a thumb spike, anything.

They didn't.

My head cleared and I moved slowly, looking around.

The Iguanodons were ignoring me. My best guess was they realized I wasn't a threat. I stood up carefully and spotted the hatch. I also saw that the raptors were climbing back up to their "posts" overlooking the valley.

I was grateful that they hadn't attacked, that I hadn't been the one to set off the war between the plant-eaters and the meat-eaters. On the other hand, I couldn't understand why they hadn't done it. What were they waiting for?

The red-ringed raptor stood on the ridge where I had been watching them before. The smashed tree where I had been hiding was at his back. He was making some kind of sound, and the raptors were retreating.

A dinosaur brushed against me. I almost jumped, but I didn't.

It was Iggy. He didn't look my way. I have no idea if he recognized me.

Growls came from the bigger dinosaurs. I moved away from Iggy and the growls stopped.

I made it to the hatch and yanked on the metal ring. The door was heavy and there was rust around the hinges. I pulled until the muscles in my arms felt like they were tearing—and it came open.

A shaft of darkness waited in the open hatch. Using the flight of metal stairs, I climbed down into it.

CHAPTER 15

I reached the bottom of the stairs and turned on my penlight. It was stuffy and hot in the small chamber. A heavy metal door sat three feet in front of me. A shiny silver plate was on the wall next to the door. The specs said it was a heat and pressure sensor. Putting your hand on it and pressing it activated the heat scanner. A typical human being's heat signature would open the door.

I was breathing hard as I put my hand on the sensor and pushed.

Nothing happened.

I licked my lips and pushed again. The plate moved a little. I heard little clicks. Whirs.

RAPTOR

Then silence.

"Come on," I said. "Come on, please."

More silence.

I pressed against the plate. I shoved and I waited and I pressed again.

"Please," I whispered.

Still nothing.

I collapsed against the door—and it sprang open under my weight! I spilled into a dark room, tripping on something near the entrance. Searing, intense lights came on, and I winced. Then I heard air blowers churn like growling beasts. I laughed and picked myself up as I looked around.

The room was just like in the specs. An underground bunker—white walls, floors, ceilings, counters, and chairs. A couple of work-stations, clipboards, lockers everywhere I looked.

I heard movement from above and closed the door behind me. The same tiny clicks sounded.

I was safe.

I sat down in one of the chairs, still laughing. I saw a stack of papers and hurled them into the air as I screamed with relief! They came floating down, a few whipping around as the cold air from the vents caught them.

I did it.

I did it!

I couldn't calm down. I got up and started

going through some of the lockers. I found canned food. Supplies of fresh water. Stacks of technical manuals. Clean clothes. There were other lockers, but I stopped. Something hit me.

I looked around. Okay. So where was the communications equipment?

I saw the workstation where the radio should have been, but it was empty. The computers weren't there, either.

That was weird. I found electrical plugs and phone and coaxial jacks.

I went through the lockers again. Two pretty big ones at the end were locked. I relaxed. Sure. They'd keep equipment that could get damaged by dust or dirt or heat or whatever wrapped in plastic or something.

I found tools and broke open the first locker. Inside, I found a pair of stun weapons, fully charged; boxes of some sort of anti-dinosaur tear gas canisters; and some jackets and pants that were heavily padded. A recharger for the stun weapons sat on the bottom of the lockers, a rectangular gray unit with little plugs and wires.

This would be great if I was going to war, but I wasn't. I was going to send word and the rescuers were going to come. I was going to see my mom again. My dad. My friends.

I was going home.

It took a lot longer to pry open the second locker. When I finally did, I stared at what was inside for a long time.

The shelves were empty.

It just wasn't possible. I went through all the lockers again. I hunted around the floor for more storage space like I had found in the rec room.

Nothing.

I picked up the clipboard I had ignored before. The paper attached was a construction schedule. The last entry read:

Final appropriations meeting 9 A.M. Monday. Computers and communications equipment to be moved in on Tuesday. Test run scheduled for Friday. Safe house should be fully operational in one week.

The log wasn't finished. Whoever wrote the note never came back. The safe house wasn't completed. There was no way to call for help.

I sat staring at the progress log for what felt like a long time. The idea of the safe house had given me hope and kept me going. Now . . .

I went crazy. I don't know how else to describe it. I kicked lockers, I threw everything that wasn't bolted down, I broke a couple of the overhead lights, I screamed until my throat was raw. I kept on like that until the fight went out of me and I was lying on the floor, curled up, wondering why they'd given up on me, why no one would help me. . . .

After a while, I got off the floor.

Ben didn't leave me because he had wanted to. And I knew my parents wouldn't give up on me. Not ever.

There's always a way. My dad had said that. Come to think of it, so had Ben.

I looked around again. The recharging unit for the stunner was a portable generator. I remembered the radio I'd found at the compound.

If I could wait out what was happening above and get this unit out of here and back to the compound—

Suddenly, the lights started flickering. The air shut off.

I ran to the door and slammed my hand against the pad on my side. I waited for the clicks. This time, the only thing that came was darkness.

CHAPTER 16

The pad didn't work. I pressed it and punched it and kept yanking at the heavy door handle, but it just wouldn't give.

I was trapped. I didn't know how long the air would last. This place was sealed off, like a bomb shelter. The air came from an independent supply somewhere on the other side of one of the safe house's walls.

I had to use my head. I couldn't afford to panic. Turning on my penlight, I went to the locker with the stun weapons. It didn't take much to learn how they worked. They were shaped like rifles, with barrels that were long metal tubes. There were four levels of intensity and a trigger to set the weapon off.

IGUANODON

One squeeze of the trigger, and electricity flared along the barrels, a flow of white, searing sparks.

I used a weapon's handle to batter the lock panel off the wall, exposing a mass of wires and metal leads. I shoved the barrel in and squeezed the trigger.

An explosion of white light and a rippling jolt of electricity sent me flying back. The lights flickered for a second, and I heard the roar of the generators. Then the room was dark and silent again.

My hands were tender, like they'd just been scalded. I used my elbows and knees as I got up and fell against the door. I hadn't heard the clicks of the lock. Drawing a deep breath, I stood back and pulled at the door.

It opened. Fresh, cool air flooded the dark room. But my relief disappeared fast.

The hatch was open up above. Raptors could have gotten in. I didn't see anything in the small hallway, but it was dark and would have been pitch black if not for the little bit of golden light coming in from above. It was dawn.

I took off my shoe and used it to keep the door open. Then I went back to the locker and got the other stunner. I had it set and ready, propped against a table.

I tore off my poncho of leaves and slipped on

the protective gear I'd seen. It was hot, the pads were thick, and there was enough room in the jacket for two of me. I pulled it tight and used some straps with buckles I'd found to keep it close to my body so it wouldn't limit my movements.

There were safety goggles and a helmet, too. Kind of like a football helmet with a grid over the face. The pants were way too big, too roomy and too long. I tried using my knife to cut through the pants, but I couldn't pierce the fabric.

That was good, considering what I had in mind.

I filled my pockets with the tear gas canisters and slung my bag over my back. At the door, I got my shoe back on. I must have looked like that kid in *A Christmas Story* whose winter parka was so bulky that when he fell in the snow, he couldn't get up. But I could move. I had to. It was the only way I'd survive.

I left the safe house with the small but really heavy generator. I kept the stunner under one arm and awkwardly climbed to the top with the generator. I nearly fell twice.

I thrust the barrel of the stunner through the open hatch. Nothing tapped it. Nothing got curious.

I climbed out and saw amber and red streaks low in the sky. The sun could only barely be seen between the branches of the trees in the east.

The Iguanodons paced nervously. I spotted Iggy and slowly walked his way. I didn't make any sudden or threatening movements, and none of the bigger dinosaurs tried to stop me.

I stopped before Iggy and hoped he would hold still for what I had in mind. He looked at me suspiciously. Then I took out the last candy wrapper I had left. He recognized the scent. My scent.

I had led him to food once. I hadn't hurt him. And he'd saved my life.

He made the mournful cry I'd heard last night. I thought of Ben and made the same sound in return.

He came a little closer.

"I can't carry this thing," I said as I set down the generator. "Not if I'm gonna get us out of here."

I pulled a long length of cord from my bag.

"I know you don't understand a word I'm saying," I said. "But, um . . . I just need you not to get freaked here, okay?"

Iggy just kept watching me. My heart was thundering. I saw movement from the raptors on the ridge. The big one with the red rings was making some kind of hollow sound.

"Okay," I said. "I'm talking to a dinosaur, and it's not even *close* to the craziest thing I'm gonna do today."

I draped the cord over Iggy and pulled it around. A couple of the bigger Iguanodons came closer. They towered over us.

I put the generator on Iggy's back and secured it with the cord.

Three more Iguanodons moved in menacingly. Protectively.

Good. That's what I was counting on.

"They said birds are all that's left of the dinosaurs," I told Iggy in a sudden burst of nervous chatter.

I tied another cord in place. Then another.

"My dad would probably say that was crazy—"

The other Iguanodons were surrounding me now. I tried to see past them to the raptors on the ridge.

"He has this thing about playing it safe. He doesn't know much about adapting to change. And my friend Ben, he just expected the world to change for him. And it did, a lot of the time. Just not when he came here."

I stepped away from Iggy.

"Adapt or perish," I said. "That's what Dr. Grant said it all comes down to. I think that's what's going on with the raptors. There's too many of them. Too many meat-eaters. And not enough meat. They're going hungry, so they trapped you guys to pick you off a little at a time. But they're not smart enough to see there isn't enough food for all of you. When you get sick, when you starve . . ."

I knew what would happen, but I couldn't say the words. The war would come. The big battle I thought I was going to see last night. But by then, it wouldn't be a fight. Just a slaughter.

I turned away from Iggy and slowly moved away from the herd. I walked toward the ridge where the alpha male raptor stood. There was a nice, easy slope right there. Perfect for Iggy and the herd to travel up to get out of the valley and find food again. *If* they were willing to fight.

I was gambling my life on what my instincts were telling me—that they *were* willing to fight.

I set the stunner for the maximum charge and headed toward the gathering raptor clan.

CHAPTER 17

There's nothing in the world exactly like walking right up to the head of a raptor clan. It doesn't feel like it's you doing it. The idea's so crazy, you figure it's got to be someone else who's actually moving to challenge the predator. You're just watching from somewhere else, somewhere safe.

RAPTOR

Only *you're* the one who's being watched.

Back in Enid, I had faced the biggest, baddest defensive line in the county on the Temple Hills Lions football field. But then I had my whole team backing me.

I'd been listening for some sign that the Iguanodons were coming with me. It didn't seem like they'd budged.

All of a sudden, my plan didn't sound so great. Better plans came into my head.

But it was too late. I couldn't go back.

I heard scurrying sounds on either side of me. Raptors coming in from my left and right flanks, while the leader held me with its cold black stare.

My finger went to the trigger. I wished I had both stunners, but the other one had been fried when I'd used it to open the safe house door.

I spun to my right and hit the trigger as that raptor jumped at me. The barrel fired up, and the shock made the animal spring back. The other one landed on my back, digging its claws into my protective jacket. I aimed the stunner back over my head and nailed the predator before we hit the ground. I rolled and came up with the stunner still in my hand.

Two blockers down. The lead raptor stared at me, amazed. My hand was already in my pocket. I slipped the release mechanism on the side of the canister and lobbed it right at good old big, red, and ugly. A cloud of tear gas exploded in Red Rings's face. It yipped and jumped back, its cry of pain and surprise creating a panic among the other raptors.

I ran right for the pack leader. A couple of the

closest "soldiers" closed rank around it. Another gas canister scattered them.

A gray cloud was forming around the raptors. I saw shapes darting around me, and I stunned two more raptors.

My eyes were starting to sting. I couldn't keep this up for long. The gas had been made to mess up dinosaurs, but it didn't help human beings much, either.

A raptor came out of nowhere and kicked at my side with the sickle claw of its right foot. I heard a rip and felt a sharp sting as the impact spun me around and I fell. I landed on my back and another raptor pounced on me. The stunner was wedged between us, its red-hot barrels less than an inch from my face.

I couldn't take out the raptor without frying myself.

The raptor's claws tore into the pads of my jacket, leaving deep gashes. I thought of the sash I'd used to hold the oversized jacket together. If it was slashed, the jacket would fall open and I'd be dead.

I shoved with all my weight, pushing at the raptor as it bit and caught on the barrels of the stunner. I smelled his breath as I shoved one last time and hit the trigger.

It was a short blast. The raptor was flung back, broken teeth flying, and sparks hit my face, burning me.

I was back up, looking for the pack leader, trying to get my bearings.

I looked to the valley and saw the Iguanodon herd stampeding—in the *other* direction.

I'd thought they'd see the raptors as vulnerable and join my fight. But I'd thought wrong. Maybe that was what *human beings* would have done. But these were not humans. They were frightened animals.

At least a dozen raptors raced after the fleeing plant-eaters. I ran back down the slope, knowing there was no chance I could reach the Iguanodons before the crazed bunch of predators attacked them. My only hope was that I could even the odds and help to keep Iggy and the generator he carried safe.

Suddenly, the raptor leader sprang in front of me. It hissed and growled so loudly that I hit the trigger of the stunner before it was even in range.

Nothing happened. It jumped at me and I swung the stunner at it.

I missed. It was on me, driving me back to the ground, claws raking across the helmet I wore. One of its claws caught in the face grid, and it wailed as it tried to free itself. I yelled as the sharp claw sliced back and forth centimeters above my eyes. My head was yanked back and forth, and I thought my neck was going to break. Then the raptor freed itself, ripping the faceplate loose.

"Agh!" I hollered, jumping back and away from the predator. It came again and I struck out with the stunner.

The weapon connected—and one final charge ripped along its barrels. Crackling white-hot energy hit the raptor, and it went down.

The other raptors stopped before they reached me. They looked at their leader, who lay still at my feet.

I grabbed another canister, primed it, and lobbed it at the startled predators. It exploded and they scattered. As the cloud of gas drifted my way, I saw something on the ground: the raptor's sickle claw, broken clean off.

I grabbed it and headed down the valley.

I had wanted to break the alpha male's hold on the pack and create chaos so the Iguanodons could escape.

I'd half succeeded. Only a couple of the Iguanodons had reached the top of the opposing rise before the raptors reached them. The rest were battling the predators, who tore and slashed and had already brought down two of the larger dinosaurs.

By the time I got there, another had fallen.

I lobbed canisters of tear gas and picked off what raptors I could. Soon, most of the Iguanodon herd had reached the top of the rise, abandoning the wounded. All but three of the raptors ran down to feast on the fallen. The others tried to startle the larger animals and find the smallest and most vulnerable. Thinning the herd. That meant Iggy.

I saw him near a huge tree. The bigger Iguanodons who had been protecting him were nowhere in sight. I had the terrible feeling that they had been among the fallen.

Two of the raptors were closing on Iggy. I couldn't understand at first why he wasn't running. I thought he was just afraid. Then I saw that the nylon cord I'd used to secure the generator to his back had been snagged on a low, heavy branch.

The generator itself looked as if it had been hit with a sledgehammer. Metal and wire streamed from a cavity in its center, and some kind of fuel leaked out of a shattered cell at its core.

I stopped. The two raptors racing toward Iggy didn't. They didn't understand that the reason I had done all this had been destroyed. They couldn't understand the ice running through me at the thought that I had failed. They wouldn't have cared if they did.

The animal part of my brain told me to run. Just run.

Run as far and as fast as I could and hope nothing caught me.

Run for the rest of my life with this moment at my back.

A memory flashed into my head. Ben caught in the harness. Hanging from the tree. Battered. Broken. Trying to smile. Trying to reassure me even though he must have sensed it was over for him—that his injuries were fatal.

There was nothing I could do.

Not then.

My hand went to my pocket. I dug out another canister, primed it, and lobbed it in Iggy's direction.

Then something slammed into me from behind and brought me down.

The third raptor. Its claws dug into the padding on my back and sides. It grabbed at my arms and raked its claws on the helmet I wore with the sickening sound of nails on a chalkboard, only worse.

It slashed again, and I felt something give around my chest.

The sash! It had torn open the sash. The dinosaur dug its claws into the padding, and I dropped the stunner and dragged myself ahead, my arms dangling at my sides. The raptor yanked the jacket right off me.

I got up, grabbed a rock, and threw it at the confused animal. It ran off, its claws still stuck in the jacket.

Then I heard a mournful wail.

Iggy.

I stumbled into the cloud of gas. Shapes blurred past me as my eyes teared up. I saw Iggy frantically struggling. The raptor claw was in my hand, and I sawed at the nylon cord. It frayed and broke, letting him run free, the shattered remains of the generator dropping to the ground.

I fell against the tree, heard screeches from below, and saw a branch I could grab. I climbed until I knew I was well out of reach of the remaining raptors.

Safe for now, I put my hands over my stinging eyes and waited for the sounds of the battle below to finally end.

CHAPTER 18

It took a day for the raptors to leave. I had time to think while I waited. Looking back on everything, I realized that what I *thought* wasn't really important. What mattered was what I *felt*.

Ever since I'd come to the island, I'd either played it safe or taken risks. Gone the way of my father or my friend. That wasn't going to change. But I hadn't felt like I was a part of things here. How could I?

I'd been running. I'd been hiding.

I stared at the raptor claw. Looking at it, I *knew* that I had finally learned Dr. Grant's lesson. I had adapted. I had become a part of the island and it had become a part of me.

While making my way back to the compound, I stopped for the night, safe in the branches of a high tree. I watched the sun

set, a fiery golden pearl hovering in the center of the far horizon. The trees before me were black, perfect silhouettes, the distant hills a soft burnt umber against a pastel orange and blue sky.

Two forms moved on the crest of the far hill. A Triceratops and a T. rex. I was too far away to hear their confrontation. They were like ghosts rising from a mist, incredible shapes that were a part of the ever-changing landscape.

They battled. The T. rex finally backed down and ran from the Triceratops. The horned dinosaur turned and calmly walked away. Soon both shapes melted away into the ridge. It could have been a mirage. A trick of my imagination. But it had been real.

This was the beauty of the island. Nature is cruel, but it gives us a fighting chance—and, along the way, some incredible sights. I had found an amazing world to live in for as long as I had to live.

And I could accept that.

The next day, I reached the compound. On the way, I inspected that abandoned water tanker in the swamp that I'd stumbled upon. It was a place I could easily defend, and it was large enough to live in.

I decided it would be my new home.

Time stopped for me. I was now like any other animal on the island. I did what I had to do to survive. And when I ran into trouble, I used my human intelligence as a weapon the same way a dinosaur might have used its spikes or tail.

I don't know how many days or weeks passed from that point on, but one night I was on my way to the compound for supplies when I heard a voice in the night.

A *human* voice.

At first I thought I was imagining it, but I crept closer to the sound until I was certain. Yes, a man's voice!

A rescuer?

A part of me that had been sleeping for so very long woke at the thought. Hope flooded through me.

Then I heard the sound of raptors. I took to the trees and came close enough to see a man a hundred yards distant, trapped in the cracking branches of a tree just above a group of angry raptors.

My heart sank.

This man was no rescuer. *He* was the one who needed the rescue.

I fished into my bag for the last remaining tear gas canisters and leaped quietly to the ground.

I didn't yet know the man was Dr. Alan Grant. And I hadn't yet learned that my parents were not far away—and in as much trouble as he was.

As I put on my goggles, wrapped a rag around the lower half of my face, adjusted my camouflage jacket of leaves, and set off to help the man, I was certain of only one thing:

Now and forever, I was a survivor.

Don't miss the next
JURASSIC PARK™ Adventure!
PREY
by Scott Ciencin

A band of teenagers armed with video cameras and what they think are "the rules of the island" invade Jurassic Park. But their dream of making a blockbuster dinosaur documentary soon turns into a nightmare because dinosaurs don't play by anyone's rules. Can paleontologist Dr. Alan Grant and thirteen-year-old Eric Kirby save them? Or will they *all* become prey?

Coming Fall 2001
ISBN: 0-375-81290-3

ABOUT THE AUTHOR

SCOTT CIENCIN is a bestselling author of adult and children's fiction. Praised by *Science Fiction Review* as "one of today's finest fantasy writers" and listed in *The Encyclopedia of Fantasy*, Scott has written over forty works, many published by Warner, Avon, and TSR. For Random House Children's Publishing, Scott has been a favorite author in the popular DINOTOPIA series, for which he's written six titles: *Windchaser, Thunder Falls, Sky Dance, Lost City, Return to Lost City,* and *The Explorers.*

Among Scott's other recent projects is the children's series DINOVERSE, a six-book fantasy adventure that takes readers on an exciting and humorous journey through the Age of Dinosaurs. Scott's DINOVERSE titles include: *I Was a Teenage T. Rex* (#1), *The Teens Time Forgot* (#2), *Raptor Without a Cause* (#3), *Please Don't Eat the Teacher!* (#4), *Beverly Hills Brontosaurus* (#5), and *Dinosaurs Ate My Homework* (#6).

Scott has also directed for television and scripted comic books. He lives in Florida with his wife, Denise.

Adventure Is Reborn . . .

Don't miss the books based on the motion picture,
The Mummy Returns! Relive all the on-screen adventure with
The Mummy Returns Scrapbook and *The Mummy Returns*
junior novelization. And for all-new adventures,
pick up *Revenge of the Scorpion King*—the first book in the
original series, The Mummy Chronicles.

And coming soon

THE MUMMY CHRONICLES BOOK II:
Heart of the Pharaoh

FREE PC CD-ROM!

Plus $2.99 Shipping & Handling.

For the interactive adventure of your life, send away for the **JP3 DIGITAL DINOSAUR ACTION PACK**, a CD-ROM (PC Only) filled with tons of great dinosaur stuff for your computer. Or go to **www.JP3pcgames.com/demo1** and download game demo's right away!

DINO DEFENDER™

Gear up for adventure and save Jurassic Park by capturing different dinosaurs in 6 eye-popping, 3D levels. Filled with action, adventure and tons of different dinos to battle. Demo includes one full level.

DANGER ZONE!™

Go head-to-head in 15 fun Mini-Games—Battle dinosaurs and your opponent to be the first to discover the Secret of Jurassic Park! Demo includes 3 full mini-games.

 ## DINOSAUR FIELD GUIDE

An interactive preview of the **Dinosaur Field Guide**, a new Jurassic Park Institute' book from Random House Books for Young Readers. Preview includes 4 different dinosaurs.

Plus MUCH, MUCH MORE!!

HOW TO ORDER

Send a 3" x 5" postcard with name, address and phone number plus $2.99 (Canada $4.99) check or money order for shipping & handling (make check payable to Havas Interactive):

**PC CD-ROM Demo by Mail
Dept. KA5814
4247 S. Minnewawa
Fresno, CA 93725**

Knowledge Adventure®